THE CHARNEL IMP

THE CHARNEL IMP

A NOVEL BY

ALAN SINGER

NEW YORK FICTION COLLECTIVE BOULDER

1987

First Edition

Published by Fiction Collective with assistance from the National
Endowment for the Arts; the support of the Publications Center,
University of Colorado, Boulder; and the cooperation of Brooklyn
College, Illinois State University, and Teachers & Writers
Collaborative.

Grateful acknowledgment is also made to the Graduate School, the
School of Arts and Sciences, and the President's Fund of the
University of Colorado, Boulder.

Address inquiries to: Fiction Collective, c/o Department of English,
Brooklyn College, Brooklyn, New York, 11210

Library of Congress Cataloging in Publication Data

Singer, Alan.
    The Charnel Imp.

I. Title.
PS3569.I526C5   1987   813.'54   87-11859
ISBN: 0-932-51111-2
ISBN: 0-932-51112-0 (pbk.)

Typeset by Fisher Composition, Inc.

Manufactured in the United States of America

Designed by Abe Lerner

For Nora

No trace anywhere of life, you say,
pah, no difficulty there,
imagination not dead yet,
yes, dead, good,
imagination dead imagine.

Samuel Beckett

THE CHARNEL IMP

A LEOPARD-SPOTTED STEER heaved its grazing head from a pile of blue rocks and drooled the only moisture that was not piped across the land. One fell panting across the azure depth of the highway. With its horn stuck in the yellowing flank of an abandoned farm building, another stood still under the stroking hand of the sun. A man could not walk between these carcasses to record the deaths unless he stopped each time, while his feet were still planted in rootless terrain, and, sucking his own mouth out of the torrid windstream, wrung another drop from his canteen. It might flow from anyone's lips. But they are mine.

The stockyards are a labyrinth folded into the furrows of my Moertle's brain. He drives the herds through a needle's-eye opening in the square corral. He prods them through wooden alleys chewed to dust underfoot. And when he is nipped and swallowed by the shadow of the slaughterhouse roof, and when he is stepping along a certain well-known length of whitewashed fencework where no gate opens under the protuberance of the naked eye, he presses his fingers against the invisible toothmarks of a

11

saw and makes the planking sway. Then tearing his eyes away from the silken horns, pulling the fence apart with his hands—a thrust of the electric prod curdles the milky underbelly—but blocking off the length of the alley with his own spread-eagle form and with a slap like a handful of minnows scattered over the pied haunch of the steer, he lets one go. On the other side of the fence the steer is free to roam into an unbounded horizon. The rest will be reduced to their hooves by the time my Moertle is washing his feet in a cooling pail of suds, stooping and waiting for the sun to crawl off his back.

The lowing of the herd fills kitchen windows, nests in the troughs of brick-red chimneys, hums through the engines of idling cars, whispers beneath the swinging skirts of waitresses and mothers, reaches into all the perspiring joints of our laboring populace like dirty fingers of soot from the two brute smokestacks, pouring off the fat of the bones in black and white and mottled clouds stampeding the slaughterhouse gates.

The liberated steer stared back through the jagged cut in the fence. Hustus Moertle thrashed his hat across his knee.

"Git." His voice was masticated in the gritted teeth of the fence as the planking swung to again, healing the gap in a wall equally splashed with whitewash and dung. Now peering over the obstacle it posed, he could see the steer rooted in place on the other side, stock-still. He knew it would be conspicuous from the humped and blackened typewriters dilating in their office windows, perched and chattering beneath the eaves of the slaughterhouse roof.

So again he shooed off the steer.

"Git."

Then: "Goat." His dog appeared on command. Moertle cradled the spotted dog against his face in a fit of impatience that seemed to gorge his mouth with fur. Then, letting fly with the dog over the fence, its feet sticking out like the spokes of a wheel, he saw it land with full momentum in the shadow of the obstinate steer.

At a distance the steer became indistinguishable from the cars that warily sniffed around it in a dry intersection of blue streets.

Later when he held the dog again between patting hands: "Blue as my own eyes," Moertle said. He patted the ground with his knees and waited for the dog to respond.

"Well, I shot you over that fence and after him you went, didn't you? You old goat. Right into the blue."

He yanked the dog's goatee like a bellpull and knocked once on the side of its head.

"Kiss."

MONOLOGUE OF THE SPOTTED DOG

Unblue. But flying. Spotted wingflap and I'm down, drowning in dust-motes, veils of gold falling over me, keeping my head under, tied to a stone, until I can see what propulsion is finally given to the steer's cast-iron hulk by glittery obsidian hooves. The scorched wind that stuck to my tongue like a burning steak congeals in the air and lands with many reverberations in the already turbulent wake of the other animal's flight: my bark is a dry bone coughed up to show this scrawny man what has

13

passed as fast as the switching of a cow's tail through the walls of my body.

The deputies' gaze hung like a string of beads between the carcass and the truckbed, glittering helplessly without a crane or harness to save their shoulders. Though its hide was a deflated balloon sucked back against the whistling rib cage, and clinging to the trelliswork of bone, the body was still weighted with the stones of its grinding existence on the open plain. It had fallen in the cul-de-sac of a caved-in feed store, seedless as an empty pod, a deserted smithy's, the vague outline of an anvil jagged in the razor-glass of one broken window, a gingerbread house of wood and a brick boardinghouse whose vertiginous rooftop jellied the excited eyes of children who leapt up its six flights of stairs the better to plummet in the long look down.

The steer had fallen with its head atop its crumpled forelegs like the first stone of a cairn marking possession on the land. The badges of the two deputies shot at each other with flaring light as they stooped to tangle their chains around the rear axle of the truck, shackling the carcass's hindhooves to the throb of the engine, watching to see if it would jump.

"Nothing for it to graze on here." The first deputy scattered his eye for whatever drooled path of animal instinct could have courted a cow of the open range to this destination.

"Don't jump!" The eyes of the second deputy were suddenly snatched up in the waving hands of children who dangled from the boardinghouse roof, their voices uplifted but their eyes starting out of their heads, with all the powdery bits of masonry crumbling to the truckbed below.

But before the deputy could take a step in the direction of the old boardinghouse one of them yelled, "Cow!" and the heads were yanked back beyond the roof rim, into the clapping hands of some unseen adult supervision. Then the woman appeared.

The rear of the animal was slightly canted, the better to mate with the red-hot pipes, clanking metal rods and prodding springs coaxing movements of an outrageous afterlife as its carcass was dragged along.

The deputies sopped hats across their brows. Their tongues mined salt from the corners of their mouths. Baubles of perspiration dangled from their ears. The flame of a woman's loosened red hair, windblown, licking the skillet bottom of the sky, would have been more than they could bear. So they did not look back to the top of the boardinghouse roof, but held their eyes like squirming fish to the ground, raised a little dust from the cracked leather seat of the truckcab, lifted their canteens to the sound of the exploding engine and were seen to trail the horns and hooves and deathless hide of the animal whose ancient herds would have washed over these tire tracks, a primordial sea.

From the rooftop, the woman who was furled in the flag of her own hair watched them go. The cries of children no longer billowed around her or stirred up the frothy hem of her gown. But beneath the tented calm of her clothing, breasts, knees and burrowing navel all wobbled on an axis of grief turning like a spit through the length of her body.

My Moertle swooned under the passionate breath of a hundred swishing cow tails when he first stood in the open hangar of the slaughterhouse entrance. His face, masked, with the dust of the trail was grateful for the cooling spigot of shadow pouring its relief from the sun. But he detested the sounds that flowed along with it, the snorting, lip-burbling lowing of the herd. In this vaulted space with its imposing heavenward reach as dark as an indrawn breath—except for nervous beads of electricity perspiring aloft—the sounds of the open range could only be magnified by corrugated aluminum walls and roof. Moertle shook his head to hear the low tremulous groan of the cattle, so lightly lifted by the pleasant prairie breezes, now so heavily piled up in the dark, into unrecognizable heaps of misshapen sound. His face showed the squeamishness of someone with an ear to the full belly of human digestion.

The most effluvial discharge of the animal lungs was not dissipated in the resonant flanks of this building: but always transformed, bred with the bellowing blows of the sledgehammer, the shocked, wet, puckering sound of burst blood tubes, gastric eruption of chains and harnesses, conveyor belts chugging along like the burden of an indigestible meal, all despite the ceaseless chomping of saws and cleavers, glinting the leanest light in the place. Moertle always ordered the hound to wait outside, fearing its bark might get caught up in the melee like a loose necktie wagging into the grip of some remorseless machinery.

The ripened lummoxes were brought to their knees on

16

the first floor of the bleeding establishment, each one
thudding its bruised equivalence to so many bushels of
apples. Though the center of the structure was open from
floor to ceiling, a wooden mezzanine traversed the perimeter halfway up. The length of the mezzanine along each
wall was there chopped up into the assembly line stations
of the butchering process.

The headless carcasses were lifted by glistening hooks
to the cutting boards above. Fatty curds of sawdust
balled up under Moertle's boots as they carried him up
too, winding along the slippery rope twine of a wrought-
iron spiral staircase. Because it was not the blood that
disgusted him. He did not flinch from the bite of steel
hooks dangling their prey from a voracious height. The
shrill sawbuzz did not invade the tenderness of his own
nose like a slender blade. His stomach did not overflow
with the glimmering buckets of burst tissue-sacs pressed
against heaving walls. Moertle had passed hours with his
own hand like a trowel against his stomach, digging out
the shape of each organ. So the lunar madness of this
slaughter could never raise a tide of sickness in him.

He continued up.

Because it was not the blood that disgusted him but
the bones. And like a victim of vertigo, Moertle could
not escape the iron grip of the topmost step, his eyes
teetering on a brink of credulity, for the first time the
pains kicking his stomach in fits—he gripped his mouth,
a throb of the heated rodent's body when it is cupped
against the wainscoting an inch away from its hole—gag-
ging, reeling and finally kneeling before the blood-blotted
mirage of a stamped and scintillating side of beef.
Chained by the hooves behind it, the rest of the herd was

17

hung in impeccable array, their aluminum racks sparkling in the eyes of white-coated inspectors patrolling the aisles up and down.

Because it was not the blood that disgusted him but the bones that stuck out now like a spoon to stir the cauldron of his brain. He knew he could never pick out a familiar tune on the keyboard of those ribs. He could no longer find any place to mount the essential horns or see how the hide could be fitted again over a basically trapezoidal form. Where was the tail to be found like a loop of discarded rope?

He had felt this panic only once before when he permitted his own body to be flung about with much centrifugal force amidst the candied lights of a carnival midway. When he was back on his feet again he felt their unfamiliar shapes beneath him and collapsed—head rolling out of the reach of his arms—to betray the transforming illusion.

But here he could not decide whether it was himself or the animal that had changed more. He tried to supply the familiarizing whistle of the prairie breeze from the purse of his pinched lips. But these bones were bent to a different wind. Shining through a translucent membrane, the long striations of eye-white suggested nothing more to him than the random pattern of red meat and wooly fat that coagulated around them and in turn pulsed their own intimations of a design that swirled and bulged but would not ever be ventilated in the lumbering strains of a loud yet gentle moan.

Now my Moertle always keeps a portion of his day for an offering to the bones, when he can stand for a few moments cursing their deformity black and blue. It matters nothing to him that he can't even hear the blows of his own speech for all the havoc of butchery, because he isn't speaking to anyone. My Moertle disapproves of the *shape* of the meat. His eyes grow fiery in the glow of its ruby facets and his voice shivers with the resistance of the inmate who will not swallow the portion of forced food. Wringing his hands so hard that the blood paints writhing pictures on his skin, my Moertle must steal his eyes away from the inquisitive white-coated inspectors, their official gaze inadvertently freezing upon him in the crisp atmosphere of refrigeration. Though his voice at such times must creep furtively back to his mouth it cannot be stilled and will only squat grumbling on the porch of his lower lip:

"I've saved a passel out, who'll not be changed. Legs remain legs, horns to the point, a belly for breath and a tail to twitch the eyes with. That's what I mean by perfect. And anyone can spoil a perfect pattern. But can you make it right? Will anything ever be the same?"

My Moertle's feet burrow distractedly in the sawdust. He shakes hands with himself behind and rocks silently back and forth, a nervous beau courting his answer from chubby cheeks and the lips of a breathtaking wound. He understands that he has only won the right to ask his question one more time. He leaves his footprints in the clean bed of sawdust, the impress of two trembling eggs.

Holding these thoughts between the uplifted intelligences of thumb and forefinger, he has never been able to squeeze the idea of the cow back into its skin.

The dark dome of the opera house hung over the town like an ancient bell ringing with the ruckus kicked up inside. Outside, a small knot of cowhands who had already spent too much time in the saddle to endure the strange grip of orchestra seats, doused their heads under one of the few remaining streetlights. At the same moment, inside, "Dinah the Damsel in Distress" lost her head to a sudden slip of the spotlight. Disapproval gushed from the audience until the tottering cyclops eye found its target again, leaping upon the bouncy voice, netting the skittery hips in sequins like fish scales, picking her up by the heels and making her whole body shimmer in the wave of applause.

The heads of the audience were scattered thinly as a bad crop of cabbages. But their enthusiasm thrust itself toward the stagelights in sprouting profusion. In the aftermath of each huzzah the voice returned, hacking through a jungle of vocal chords, sweating the song out of the thick undergrowth of her small but palpitant chest.

From his banner-draped box Moertle whistled above the applause. In his excitement he was crushing the wings of a bouquet intended for flight across the stage. His hat hung from a wall-mounted pair of longhorns, freeing his head to float wildly in the buoyant murk of tobacco and unlicensed drink. Goat, the spotted dog, sat, cocked ears at Moertle's feet. And Moertle's foot trotted to a sudden prod of the music.

When Moertle's foot struck the loose board in the boarding-house steps, the children were seesawed into the air and tumbled around him. They always came when they heard him because the song was already running from his lips, spilling into whatever ears were cupped first to catch it. The smallest ones would be lifted like grace notes into his musical stride as he sought the reverberating scale of the largest room in the building.

Lillifalura, falura lures me
la la
lo lo
Lilli, the whore . . .

These children knew it was a song made up out of their
mother's name and applauded her entrance when she came in
a veritable wind of haste, guarding the flame of her hair with
fastidious fingers.

The woman on the stage appeared changed. Drenched
in a gown of white silk, which flexed every movement
like the sheen of her skin, she flounced from one side to
the other of the darkened stage, one step ahead of the
spotlight. The spot moved in the perspiring embrace of a
stagehand, whose black eye trained upon the stage from
the furthest balcony. Upstage, the trio of bass and two
violins sat all in a row, three old crows ascratch with the
frantic puppet movements of an invisible infestation of
lice. From their chairs they emitted the light buzzing
sound of the insect horde, shredding the web of the
singer's gossamer voice.

Batti, batti o bel Mazetto
la tua povera Zerlena . . .

Anyone who could see that her feet were bare knew
she left moist prints on the dusty stage. Noticing from
fluttering toes that she was about to leap into the empty
air, a few stretched their arms out to clap.
Lillifalura opened an apron full of shamrocks to the frantic
arm-waving, the bird-pecking fingers of excitement. The cook-
ies burst into a bright powder when they came in contact with
white teeth. When all the children's faces around him were
bellied out with food, Moertle came to nest his hands like

ALAN SINGER

struggling doves in the apron. The woman smiled upon the fledgling flight of his batted eyes. But when she received his hand and, despite the warmth of his gaze, she found him counting again, using his fingers like cold dusty sticks of chalk to tabulate the record of the herd. Though his eyes strained to see the children behind him—she wouldn't let him turn his head—he was really exercising his memory. He was exerting the lobes of his brain like pumping lungs, trying to fill them with the air of calm while his eyes rioted to confirm the secret number under his tongue. He never knew positively whether his previous count was inaccurate or only subject to the subtle recalculations of time in his absence. When a first child was born Moertle shuddered at the sheer proliferation of it, as someone dribbling drink down his front.

Because he found Lilli first with his fingers it was all coming back to them now, each finger becoming heavy in its turn, stiffening under the command of a mathematical certainty. "One, two, three, four, five, six, six, six." And once Lilli's body was opened he could not close it by himself. He stammered Pandora's old regret but in the end consigned himself to the empty box as his only refuge. At first he took heart that as they swam from her body, they brought little more than the gaping life of the fishbowl, bulging through the curved glass. But now they were children. They walked upright and were capable of holding his name on their tongues like melting candy. So he visited the house less often. He visited the house with careful dereliction. As they grew, he found excuses not to recognize them. He fumbled their names on his own tongue, held the six of them as one in his nervous gaze, a tentacled mass to be squinted at through the aquarium glass, never approached.

Lillifalura's face rolled under turbulent waves of her red

22

hair. Her gaze floated in the calm of a deeper current moving steadily toward the stairs. She curled her finger in his face and drew his arms out straight as the rungs of a ladder, lifting a single question to his eyes.

"Shall we rise?"

The woman on the stage came down under a graceful wingspread of white silk. In his private box Moertle was already standing, clapping, dusting rose petals from the front of his jacket when he realized he had leapt too soon to his mark. Dinah yanked her eyes away and the chasm suddenly widened between them until the return to his seat was a mile-long plummet. He saw the scorn flare from her nostrils to make him squirm and straightened himself once more for the finale. He dried the palms of his hands on a few tatters of the national banner, hung like a bib from the front of the box. He mixed the salt of his eye with the patriots' party-colored sweat furled into its puckering seams. The violins began to swarm in the darkness while it furiously dreamed a new backdrop for the stage and the headliner wriggled out of her costume in the wings. A gargantuan chandelier threw sparks from the center of the dome, making it move like the devious pupil of a vast eye. Moertle patted his dog on the back of the head and reached behind him for his hat. In the orchestra section below, the doors from the lobby winked crookedly with the commotion of last-minute seating. The crash of a whisky bottle was heard on the twinkling aisle and a few shrill voices began to climb mutinously but on real notes to the balconies above.

Moertle remained calm in his box, until he heard the door coming off its hinges behind him and the very stagehand who delayed its repair reached in, placing the

ALAN SINGER

stiff white card of the messenger like a fallen chip of plaster onto this patron's shoulder. Moertle's spasm of recognition tumbled the card into his lap and in the sink of eddying dimness it splashed the light of its communication:

Idiota!

The light broke over the stage like an egg and caught the extended limbs of the dancer in the heavy viscosity, the pure amniotic suspension and slow movement of one yet ungestated intent.

Lilli's arms and legs seemed to be suddenly cut loose from some sinister confinement when she snapped them around Moertle's rattling frame. The door to the bedroom was held by a stiff bolt. Where the curtains fluttered out through an open window, a man would have fallen headlong from its broad tombstone sill. A clock kicked aimless seconds off the night table so that they landed in the steady footfall of a broken string of beads. Moertle's breathing began to shape itself to the swell of Lilli's chest. But when she drew herself up trying to make him feel it as a thing between them, he squeezed it out again in rhythmic convulsions.

From several floors below the children's riot became audible as some liquid layer of earth bubbling to the surface until it could almost be heard in the quivering membrane of the skin. When the bolt popped out of the door it might as well have hit Moertle in the head he was so stunned to find himself in the midst of his rampaging children.

The flame from Lilli's hair was burning up her face. Moertle's spine coiled like a roused snake in her hands. But when they were both covered again, two heaving mountains raised beneath the patchy quilt, their sudden eruption set the chil-

24

dren's whitening eyes and flagged hands spinning in a widening circle of chaos. Moertle flailed from the bed like a man caught up to his waist in mud but his voice reached them with short stubby blows and herded them back down several flights of stairs on two knobbed and hairy legs of gruffness. Moertle's lungs marched from his chest to drive the invader from every corner of the room. But with his very last sweep around the bedposts, wind met rain in the stormy gaze that suddenly hung as a cloud between raging father and cowering child. The tears streamed behind as the child crawled out from under the bed, pulling seanets away from the face with frantic hands. The child's fat knees squeezed out of short pantlegs in two gouts of soft dough where it stood. Then, hands deeply socketed into eyes, the whole body pumping like an exercised heart, the child opened its mouth and bellowed back.

When Moertle heard this he choked his own voice, making the red blanket tremble in his hands, an unintentional flourish of the toreador's cape. The child lowered its head, but instead of horns let down two loops of braided hair. Two nooses for the father's unspectacled eyes as they swelled with recognition:

"What is your name, girlie? I thought you were my boy."

"I'm Myrtle too."

The music heaved behind the dancer's breast, though not a single string of her body was plucked with movement. The spotlight was melting her skin though her body stiffened from the inside, the bones shot like spears of an ice cube through her translucent pose. She was tented in an airy white gown that seemed to breathe under the lights until it had absorbed enough to reveal the body as an X-ray silhouette within; but its folds hung as straight and as stiff as the pillars of a temple. Only a card-

25

board sun and a painted tree as thin as a wafer swung to
the beat of the music, since both were dangled by ropes
from a towering height to the stage below. But the attention of the audience was so fixed they could not doubt
that the movement was theirs. They were wrapped by the
twining chords of the impassioned string trio, hauled in
on the ropes of a steady beat, until those were cut by the
roll of a snare drum boiling up as if from some invisible
crouching hole under the floorboards of the stage and
suddenly pricking the dancer alive. The tented gown
gasped between Dinah's legs. The violins were beaten
down under the steady blows of the drummer. Dinah's
legs strutted out to the sides as if to pull the vellum of her
now unwrinkled gown as taut as the drumhead. Her feet
peeked beneath the riffling hem of the gown with the
short blind leaps of jumping beans. Her arms stretched
out from her waist. They stiffened until the hands met in
an arc over her head and then her whole body, chained
up by that gesture in a dungeon of diminishing light,
began to buckle as though the rioting drumsticks were
grown to the proportions of cudgels. Dinah's head rolled
precariously on her shoulders and her knees began to
punch through the loose gown until Moertle understood
from the way her limbs held together under such a mer-
ciless beating, that she was only dancing again—but as he
had never witnessed before.

With one finger she hooked the hem of her gown and,
in perfect synchrony with the silvery ratchet of the snare
drum, the geared and pullied movement of her arm hiked
the hem of the gown to the middle of her chest. It was
lifted at just the height above her sharply scissored legs to
account for a pebble in the pool that made her mounded

Venus jump, and splashed a drop of poison in her Moertle's eye.

The lights went out when Moertle closed his eyes.
When the audience snapped the chains of decorum that
had restrained them from vaulting to the stage at once,
the abrupt movement threw Moertle off balance. It set
his eyes spinning in the featherless whirlwind of his old
vertigo. From his privileged box he felt he had been
plucked aloft in the beak of some flying gargoyle of the
upper balcony and was now being dangled over the stage
like a worm over the chirping nest. So my Moertle put
his foot down firmly in the dark and he turned his back
on the embarrassing convulsions of the stage. He wiped
the poisonous droplet from his eye and left the door to
the box open behind him, unhinged as the lid of the vam-
pire's kist.

Under the flapping wing of this departure the dog
bayed like a wind.

MONOLOGUE OF THE SPOTTED DOG

He stepped on my tail. Underfoot, now a log rolling
him off balance but stinging me like the grease pressed
out on a hot griddle, a stack of bricks rising hot as a
chimney on top of my twisting tail—now flat as the head
of a cobra and now convulsive with the venom of its own
bite. The sound flying out unscratched over my teeth,
arced through the quilted blackness like a tear in the
shroud through which the silver hatchet-nose and worm-
furrowed lips of this scrawny man's smile, shone wriggling.

27

Through the hall-lighted proscenium of the opera box door this bright tableau: the man on his knees soothing my tail between palms and rubbing faster as applause dies from within.

When the whistle blew over the slaughterhouse roof, its silver tongue gleamed into the horizon like the chain from a policeman's chest. The blue breast of the sky was already stooping to investigate a few small geysers of dust coughed up from crowded corrals as they were bolted for the night. Under the spinning silver star of an adjacent windmill, the whine of gruesome machines was throttled by the stiff fingers of the corrugated roof. Inside, the hands of the workers floated like dying fish in aluminum wash troughs. The water, pumped by the windmill, blushed with the titillation of so many dirty fingers and willingly carried away the evidence of their crime in a bloody tide that stained the copper drainplates blue. And as the flanges of the windmill began to sing against the basso gusts of a westerly wind, the throated darkness of a nearby narrow street of the town could be heard gulping down a vast silence flooded over the outlying plain.

The streets that lay sprawled behind it, breathless as any man laid flat in the ring, did not stir as if the night were only a blurred aura in the orbit of puffy eyes, or a painful weight settling uneasily in the foggy center of the brain. When a town dies, the necrophiliac throb of a few lonely footsteps on tombstone pavements taunts the pulse of its former life. It causes an abrupt tug on the puppet strings of reflex still entangling the lives of the remaining inhabitants. A hand goes out. The head nods, the corners of the mouth pull wide. In the wake of these encounters, the strings slacken, leaving the friends to twitch lifelessly at midnight behind their trembling panes of glass. Looking out.

For the wind still hurls itself against the transparent shield of our eyes, all the faster and harder now since, for over nine years, it has not borne the swelling burden of rain, the downpour kicking its heels into crusty sod, making it heave. All the silos steepling our horizon have yellowed to a ripeness once reserved for the grain that filled them up. A sickly color has come out onto the tongue of wasted prairie land that stretches listlessly away from my window. Even my corpses will yellow in their beds or on the griddled pavement before I can put down the mournful black receiver and collect the instruments for a positive diagnosis of death's cause. Even the coroner—I have outlived my years of doctoring—will be too late to beat the palsied hand of the wind that draws a dusty veil over everything that has ceased to move in this region of the world. My first duty then must always be served by snapping a bone-white handkerchief in the startled faces of the departed or parting the lips to see if they really weren't smiling under that veil. And because the farmers have all been squeezed out of the tightening fist of this land—the streets of the town thinned like grass—I am now called more often to witness a hoof that will never touch earth again than to pry the boot from a filthy white foot.

And these days a dead steer might turn up anywhere as if it had been released from the barred gates of the horizon and driven to a blue intersection of streets or an aromatic storefront by some nearly human instinct conditioned out of the wooden water trough. We find them with sides caved in, unable to move, eyes floating in a mirage, lolling tongues as fat as melons. And they might have lumbered down any one of the narrowing byways that twine together in our midst and spiral off again in as many different directions as were first summoned by the specter of multistoried buildings, confetti lights, the web of threaded power poles all roused inexplicably out of the doldrums of this flatland—the deferred dream of the sleepless herdsman wandering perilously on its rim. They might have ambled down any one of the narrowing paths or byways that intersect our lives here on the paved crosshairs of fate except there is no longer a herd, a ranch or even an occupied farmhouse for over one hundred miles in any direction. There is only the railroad that feeds itself on the endless regurgitation of its own tracks. Our ears are plugged with the single groan of the boxcars unloading their daily cargo of fattening haunch and rib. And so we sleep on in routines of the only work left for a man whose legs are bowed in an empty embrace: the whetstone and the blade. The old turf riders have dismounted to sidewalks that must be shared with the ploughman and his wife. Now all of them are followed into the gates of daily employ by the loyal herd dog, red-coated and worn but its snout still dangling from a familiar scent that blows off the empty plate of the horizon well above his master's head.

So the slaughterhouse roars all day in its chains and belts. At night the opera house can still make a noise strong enough to ring out the chambers of a workingman's heart. Our feet still tickle the sidewalks, rippling through the touch of hand to hand when we meet, raising a voice from the flesh like a bucket from the dried-up well. And we have cars and wagons for rattling the streets, a whole hive of electricity buzzes continually up above and the whistle from the slaughterhouse roof sets its shrill spark to the air three times daily. So if someone wading alone into the wide circumference of the open plain should cock one white ear like an open mouth snared on the fishhook of dark distances, if someone with one foot tossed out like a sounding stone in front of him is listening, then he must know: we are here.

The two deputies and the fat man pinched by his own vest lifted their feet into the air until they flew with spreading arms, while the dusty ground puffed vigorously beneath them. But still the birds did not take wing with rapid brushstrokes that might have spared them the sight of a cracked and sagging cowhide viciously sewn by the talons of a scavenging instinct. Rapier-beaked, haughty-shouldered triumvirate, the vultures had to be shot, still fastened to their tedious needlework before the steer's carcass could be examined for the cause of death. The feathers ruffled in death throes. Although the air-shattering wings and bellowing breasts plucked strenuously at intractable talons, only the black quills finally exploded into the air and, ink-soaked, sank back to mottle the unblemished hide of the cow. A pair of wirecutters was handy to sever the birds just above the rooted hooks.

The coroner's black bag made small noises beside the cow's hulk until all the instruments had been extracted into the light.

"Starvation," he stressed with his tongue, as if clicking the case shut. "Must have gone round here in circles for a long time before he got dizzy. A cow can't eat the sticky-weeds that grow up in the cracks of pavement, can he?" His eyes lumbered around the perimeter of the cul-de-sac butting up against boarded entrances, veering from a gashed window, turning on the white haunch of protruding vision the weight of his gaze, away from blocked alley and back again to face the blind recesses of shadow which bred spontaneously on the opposite side of the moon-shaped court.

"This street is supposed to be closed." The deputy's boot was pointing into the sunken cow's belly before he heard a second truck drive up. When the brakes were squeezed the deputy retracted his foot from an egg-shaped sand print just starting to warm between the straight legs of the carcass.

"Well, Hustus Moertle, what do you say?"

The stock warden got out beating his hat. He plucked a few stiff hairs from the embroidery of horn and hoof cleft by a red cleaver and welted with heavy thread onto the fading denim breast of his jacket. The lanky cowhand dropped his eyes into the sand like spent cartridges. But his sight never lowered from the question mark beading up over the deputy's hot face.

"I'm sure it's one of ours, Nifty," said Moertle without pausing.

The dog followed him out of the truck. They all watched the dog's nose leave a slime trail down to one hoof where it picked up the color of the cow—onyx pearl—like a secretion around the tiny grain of its scent.

"Am I right, Goat?"

32

The excited nose flowed into the air, rubbed by the raw silk of the breeze. After that leash-length spout of instinct, the dog's ear gave place for its hind foot to stand on fleas and scratch itself.

The deputy gouged the bright tablets of a tiny notebook with a mechanical pencil, then replaced it behind one ear as if swatting the wings of a few soft-spoken words.

"Well, ain't that good enough for us?" The other deputy pulled his head out of the inverted bell of his Stetson. His face remained hovering over the damp rim of the hatband. His eyes moved with the creeping leg action of any insect over a scummy surface. "Well, I'd say it's all yours, Moertle. What's your aim to do with it?"

There were children on one of the surrounding rooftops. But no one noticed the bobbing heads filled like helpless balloons with the air of that altitude.

"But it's no use to us as it is, is it?" Moertle thought if he disturbed the cowhead its ears and nostrils might be evacuated by a colony of angry ants. Moertle hoofed around to the listless coil of tail hanging his head at the opposite end of the carcass. He began to chew the cud of this problem. He wanted to drool onto the bald knuckles of the deputy's hand. He gripped his own between his teeth, one by one holding each in its turn, letting them drop one by one like pearly wisdom from the mouth.

"Listen, Nifty, I need a rope, don't I?"

The deputy reached into the lair of bald tire-and-tool chest to snatch a thrashing rope end from the dry bed of the truck. Two fang marks bled from his wrist, flicked by an open latch of the tool chest.

The noose went easily around the head of the cow.

33

Then the coroner's breath hung weightlessly on the deputy's ear. His eyes ricocheted from the cow to the stooping cowboy, sounding, in the thick pillow of his brain, the words he wanted to shout from his suffocated lungs.

But it was a sight for which there could have been no adequate warning. The coroner knew that in the breathless instant of surprise the heart squeezes all the blood into the head, not to be held accountable. He felt the blood gorging his tongue too thick for speech.

Because, before them all, Moertle had taken up his end of the rope and, never turning around to face the carcass again, he lashed it over his shoulder, secured it with the knot of his own clenched fist, leaned his whole body like a swimmer into the rising pool of road dust and proceeded to tow this cargo through the only opening in the crowd. The first tug stretched the skin smooth across the coroner's brow, yanked the corners of the deputy's smile into spittle-poisoned darts. The obstinate talons of the birds popped loose like eroded root systems from the rippling hide. But the carcass did not move.

It flaunted a mountainous prerogative that nonetheless did not interfere with the stately motion of Moertle's own feet adrift in pantomime distances.

With hands clapped over squeamish ears, warding off an explosion, plump eyes squeezed to juicy slits, backs beginning to turn their deflecting shields against the spray of sand from Moertle's feet, the small crowd implored him to let go. But Moertle's seedy eyes were scattered in the opposite direction, rope taut, his shoulder humped and ruffled with vulturous poise over an open view of the street, waiting for pigeons to descend.

The head of the cow surged with a sea that was already soaking through the hide, brimming at the shoreline of expectation. Then the tongue was cast up with the flexing of some unfathomable tidal muscle. It wriggled in the dust. The spectators gasped to see it so nakedly out of its element, licked helplessly by the darting light.

The expression on Moertle's face was pulled tight as a stocking over the nose and mouth of his breathing intent. Geysers of dust spouted from the turmoil of his now running feet. His back and shoulders pumped for an arduous lover who had slipped beyond his reach.

The cow suddenly acquired another neck where the noose bit hardest into the heavy hide, trying to pull it out of the grip of boulder-humped shoulders and fisted flanks, all still reposing as tranquilly and as belligerently behind the floating face of bovine distraction as the unintelligible rump that grips the head of the sphinx in its powerful claw.

The dog's bark lifted on dirty wings to caw down upon the calamity.

And then nobody saw what struck the cowboy to his knees, the knees beginning to dance against the ground, the rope still hauling against the dredge of the animal's heart. But something had happened to his face. It was softening like wax between the rapid modeling fingers of sunlight.

Though the eyes of the crowd hung open windows around him, Moertle could see nothing until the moment when his own eyes dilated to form thick magnifying lenses of grief. They bubbled and flowed and finally broke the surface of his concentration like the dead eyes of fish floating.

"What the hell! Look at him crying tears," the coroner shouted over the tip of one stiff finger pointing it, driving it in front of him like a spike to split the shivering nerves of the rope—Moertle let it sag at last—the space contracting in a telepathic spasm between two muscular heads.

The cowboy fell back upon the heaving carcass. But the froth of the cowboy's white eyes and the horns of the cow bobbed together on a wave that ebbed so quickly from the spectator's view that the coroner and a deputy dove with a thud onto the exposed shoal of Moertle's struggling arms and legs. Neither of them could pull the rope end out of the herdsman's grip. Together all three of them flexed the gritty joints of a tide-stranded crab. Finally Moertle felt the rope slither away from his neck, his back hoisted and cracked between two pincer knees that held the deputy boisterously astride the bucking cowboy.

The children's heads, pricked by the bobbling points of their own eyes, exploded on the rooftop overlook. The bright cloth of their throng shredded with movement— tatters flapping violently about the hips of an invisible body. Through it all a woman's white arms were waving—frantic body caught in an ill-fitting gown—until her head tore into view from the broken ring of leaping children.

The crowd below remained oblivious to everything but the sound of the deputy gargling syllables of a bitter imprecation. Their attention draining around him, the oglers hauled the lawman out of the fray—the weight of a man who had just plunged into a well—by the feet. The coroner's tentacled belly floated in the opposite direction. He sat up and wiped his face with a handkerchief. Moertle alone sank to the bottom of everyone's gaze, rock-heavy, gasping for no air, only waiting for the first damp clots of earth to lap houndishly back to his face: soft nose-lengths of excremental loam and dark-dumpling eyes packed into one skin with him at the bottom of the grave.

"Why don't he move?" The deputy hefted his belly into the air and stood over the cowboy as if he were prepared to hurl the first stone. But he turned instead so that his shadow wheeled away from the cowboy's face as portentously as from the mouth of a cave. What was revealed there took a few fledgling flutters of life upon the tearful blinking of Lilli's eyes as she who had flown from the rooftop in one movement swooped down beside the effigy of her husband.

And so Moertle was revived. Lilli's hand lit from his face. He coughed until the voice leapt, a struggling prisoner inside his throat. The coroner knelt stealthily as a poacher after the pulse scurrying along Moertle's arm. He picked it up between pinched fingers, rolled it on his thumb to ascertain perfect roundness, and dropped it back into the gullet of a throbbing artery. He watched the cowboy's arm begin to stir with all the satisfaction of one who administers the restorative pill.

Eventually, the head of the cow was swallowed into a cloud of dust, belching storm of the deputy's dented pickup, digging in with all the talons of its raspy gearbox to get a grip on the ark-ribbed carcass and drag it off its fateful grounding. But its true weight was as deceptive to the dust-swollen eye as its size would be in the contracting iris of a vulture's overcircling vigil.

In the sea-filled sac of Moertle's vision he floated, tremulously aware of the ripening teardrops even after the sun picked them off his face like fat sucking flies.

Inside the warp of a clear droplet, the ground hangs upside-down until it plops from the faucet, remembered only in the wetness of the eye that has blinked. "Look for true resemblances in the drop of water," Moertle murmurs to himself, licking the sound of the words until it fills his mouth with enough water to irrigate the fields of memory. His eye opens and his nose closes in reverie.

A boy crouched in a deep wave of grasses, the red in his face fixed fiercely as the ravaging of a surprised lioness. His lips flutter their broken wings in the taut web of the breeze. The soft centers of his eyes are stirring with some fetal life, pecking the twin yokes of vision. The bubble inside his nose heaves with a dream of its moist green sleep. The wave of grasses crests and falls on a perfect view of someone's neatly laid picnic blanket. The sky falls on it too, shut so soundly the boy's ears ring with silence, the azure pane so bright and hard it bears the full press of the child's nose.

There the boy's attention gathers like breath on cold glass. The woman on the picnic blanket is gently moistened by the child's eye. The clothes she should be wearing stir themselves in a pile beside her bowing form and the sun comes crouching monstrously behind to lick her dry. Her skin is milk on the lips of all this suspiring sunlight. The boy sees that the woman is being a mother to the infant nibbling her heart. She cradles her child in white arms. Her heart is white and hairless as the baby's head but makes no sound. And neither does the boy make a sound even to clear the lump in his throat. The lump becomes a knot when he tries to pull away, making of his gaze an entanglement that he realizes will not come easily unraveled.

And so he is tied to his vision of the blanket, the baby, the bare bowing form of the woman. As his gaze deepens, the knot bites deeper into the skin of his palpitating throat until once again he feels the wetness of his own eye with the tidal intensity of his gaze, until he realizes the tears are coming out all over his body. It is a sudden rain shower.

The first drops pricking the woman out of her trance send the boy reeling several steps backward into the trough of another grassy wave. But as he falls, eyes bright flotsam on the cresting motion of the moment, he feels his shoulders caught up not in the soft embrace of watery grasses but in the leaping eyes and blinking nostrils, the rearing surprise of a startled cow.

Its heavy head plunged to the ground, its firmly planted forehooves suddenly eroded from the shores of contemplation, the animal shudders, blows and steers off in the opposite direction, emitting upon a lashing thread of drool the sound of the lost herd.

The scene is all water now, the child making turbulent swimming movements in the animal's wake. The woman, clutching her baby like another part of herself, is amazed to see a hatless child running after the cow as quickly as though there were a kink of the animal's own springy tail in the boy's kicking legs. The woman can see the boy casting the net of some well-studied herdsmanship over the zagging path of the cow. The poor animal, with its

39

head thrown out in front of it at every gallop, as if the body could be expected to find its own way, bellows and kicks.

When the woman is able to rise and stand above the stalks of tall grass, she can see how quickly the boy has harried his prey. Standing so small in front of the cow that he might be the trough out of which it drinks, the boy is now holding the animal's head in his arms. On his lips, wet as her own field of vision, the woman detects the slow contractions of a song starting to move, an insect struggling against an invisible pane of glass.

The infant, caught in the wet grip of motherhood, is swayed by the rhythms of his mother's cradling arms. The cow does not move. Its tail now holds the tension of the electrical storm that is straining muscular dark clouds overhead. The boy is shrinking, pulling the head of the cow gently into his lap until the animal is virtually grazing over the small, crouching, sibilant figure of this pastoral world.

Moertle remembers the smell of sour grass that rose from the dark wells of the cow's eyes. His face was rippled by an expulsion of living breath from the looming nostrils. Bored with darkness and ringing with the sound of some deep burrowing life, they hovered over him.

And when he opens his eyes, Lilli's face beats down to him on gentle wings of light. The teeth of her smile shine wide with the credulity of a young girl gazing for the first time upon the hastily unfurled map of her lover's skin.

MONOLOGUE OF THE SPOTTED DOG

My master has melted right away to his feet until he is a slick puddle licking the sunlight off the sky in one smooth stroke. Now he knows the sufferance of the stubborn leash. Soon he may be acquainted with the boot. Will he drag himself forward on all fours in order to escape? To whom does he owe obedience if not himself? He does not move. Is that his answer?

But he is such a skinny man. If he stood up the sun would shine through him like a breath of mist over water. Let me bark and it might blow him away.

The spectacle of a steer kneeling inside the widely swung stage doors of the empty opera house might have caused a passerby to ponder the inconceivable shelter of the radiant crèche, the child swaddled between the doors of an open stable.

But this miracle of bovine obeisance, its head bowed toward the back of a bare stage, between broken knees, its haunch raised like an altar behind, remained an untendered vision throughout the luminous hours of this working day. Only at night, when the first stagehands appeared to speculate on the mystery of doors ajar, did a cry go up for someone to believe: an animal from the slaughterhouse had wandered backstage and now lay dead amidst the dangling ropes and sandbagged backdrops, all the space-defying painted props of a live theatrical performance. The hand that ordinarily held the steamy spotlight now tied a rope around a pair of stiffened hindhooves and stepped aside as the raspy engine of an old pickup began to exert itself in the alleyway outside. The musicians tuning their instruments in the orchestra pit fumbled with the extra notes that flowed into the theater. Their fingers groped to distinguish the stops

41

on their own horns from those that sounded with engine exhaust.

Gathered around the diffused halo of the sheriff's headlights the men responsible for mounting a musical entertainment at last saw the carcass of the steer dragged down the length of the alley and out into the street. A few straining at the ropes still breathed the odor of standing stock when the curtain went up.

"Dinah the Damsel in Distress" pulled a fistful of blue ostrich feathers tightly around her throat and bowed deeply into the beaten air of applause. Moertle moved his hands with perfect symmetry as if struggling to maintain the gasping elevations of flight. But his eyes were already falling precipitously through the circles of empty air she cut with her dancing feet. She would sing to him all night, she had promised: because the windows were shut, the floor was tight, from the walls her voice would bounce back. Tonight she swore that nothing would be lost like a trace of perfume on the flanks of expanding air that rustled in the noisy corridors outside her dressing room or strode impatiently out from under the ponderous shadow of the opera house façade into the empty street.

Seen from the street, Dinah's window held her tiny fluttering movements in a fist of light. Resuscitant with the breath of her limber body in motion, Moertle stirred in his chair, catching the feathers as they fell from Dinah's dance. Each time his hand reached out toward another feather he felt himself fall further away from the sturdy oak of the seat—until finally his arms fell fully extended upon the captive air of the room and, with his backside hovering perilously above the shrinking world of his own stiffened legs, he stood bent above the floor in a trauma of precipitous flight. Thrilled to see him so daringly outstretched on the empty air, Dinah sailed into her lover's arms and swept him into the whirlwind of her own dancing stride. The words of her song broke upon Moertle's hearing like the very thing that has dropped though no one saw it fall.

Where Moertle had fallen down in the road, he had been lifted up too and carried on the crossed arms of the sheriff and the coroner up a dizzying flight of boardinghouse stairs.

In the room, Lilli watched him from her chair. Her eyes were cast out to him in the trance of the patient fisherman, the barb of the hook clasping the tongue in silence to the roof of her mouth. A current flowed under the sleeping features of Moertle's face, tugged at the calm surface, furtively nibbled the line on which Lilli's thoughts now hung. The bed where Moertle lay did not move before her eyes. But there in the moist cleft of the mattress, Moertle himself was touched by prickly fins of consciousness and his squeamish foot shuddered up from a murky depth shaking the bed from one end to the other. (He knew the mattress springs were a fine mesh of cartilage softened in the meat of so much undulating life.)

His eyes bulged with the sensations that woke him. From beneath the lowered lids where he thought she did not yet see him, he moved to inspect the room. Because Lilli sat with her knees propped under her chin, and because her legs were long, Moertle saw her head unnatural, perched on a spike-end, the face frozen by the ice of the executioner's blade. And he heard—violently severed from his own understanding—the expulsion of grief that went from her lips.

43

*Quickly he lifted his head, tried with the movement of his
own body to shake her out of whatever dream of grief pressed
against her sleeping eyes.*

*But she had not been sleeping. She had been clenching the
secret of the child in her belly, trying to feel with vague fingers
the faint grain of life. If she told him where it lay she knew it
would begin to itch the secretions of consciousness that made of
his mind a dense pearl of obstinacy. So she let it rest in the
clamped silence of the oyster's shell.*

*But Moertle's first movement brought Lilli quickly to her
feet and then to her knees beside his bed. It seemed that she
had captured the distance between them in one stride of her
hungry legs. She pushed his naked foot back under the com-
forter. She took his arm from beneath the covers and laid it
upon a quilted field of bluebells. His foot fell out of the bed.*

*It made the sound of the dog's bone dropped between dirty
paws on the marble floor.*

"Dinah the Damsel in Distress" held her lover by the
nape of the neck and then applied him to her breast like
an asp to a queenly nipple. Moertle felt his face being
crushed against a prickly mail of tiny mirrors artfully knit-
ted into her bodice like sequins with open eyes. Her
voice sprang about the room on the whitest legs struggling to be free.

> Ma se colpa io non ho: ma se da lui
> ingannata rimasi . . . E poi, che temi?
> Tranquillati, mia vita,
> no mi toccò la punta delle dita.

But in Dinah's arms, Moertle did not struggle. Because,
where they lay embracing against the heated crimson
thigh of an overstuffed love seat, Moertle liked to feel her

throbbing against the palm of his own open hand. She was like something plucked alive out of the air and held with darkened fingers invisibly against the chest unless it would fly away. Yet when Moertle looked to see his hand moving deliberately against her belly, he saw how short was the reach of five fingers, even stretched over the bones like the face of fright.

His hand—reddened indistinguishably from the hue of her gown, the bursting blood of the velvet love seat, shiny spew of the flattened cushion—moved no more to hold her under its sway. Dinah's voice filling itself up with all the air that was left for breath in the stifling dressing room left him faint. A silent fish pucker was all his complaint when Dinah broke free from his grasp.

Then he lay beneath her as though he himself had slipped the intricate talons of the bird that carries its prey over the sharpest peaks.

Lilli let him enjoy the full weight of himself in her arms, permitting only the tail of his spine to flick silently against the mattress as she rocked him. She was telling him the story:

"Moertle appeared in a cloud of dust, walking against the tide of the taut rope that he himself had lassoed around the animal's head and slung over his shoulder like any experienced bargeman. Everyone said, 'No! Don't do that,' when Moertle took that first step into the impossible distance.

"And then the crowd inched tighter and tighter around him. But no one went close enough to pinch him out of this spell as though they were afraid there was something about the cloud of dust that had more to do with smoke from a genie's lamp than Moertle's own two feet. By then they were no longer visible in the dust they kicked up.

"Doctor Face polished his eyes with two soft knuckles of skin

45

before he could believe what he saw, because Moertle kept walking with the cow in tow and getting nowhere, like it was a man holding onto his suspenders from behind. Though everyone could see it was only a few unyielding rays of light that held him in place, a golden twine braided on ecstatic fingers of rising dust.

"Of course, it was really the cow that could not be moved. If the cow had swallowed him whole it would not have been more of a hindrance to his progress down the street.

"But no one laughed. Because that was when Moertle looked too much like a cube of ice pinched between tight fingers and acquiring from the curve of pressing thumb the quivering shape of a woman's yielding belly.

"And, sure enough, the sheriff and the doctor were wet when they finished wrestling Moertle from the snake dance of that rope. All three lay flattened on the ground as though they had fallen under the same careless footstep of gigantic sunlight.

"But you, my Moertle, lay lowest. So they needed to stoop, to bow down and to extend their arms like the doctor searching between his patient's retreating legs, when they pulled you out. And when they carried you on outstretched arms between them, Doctor Face, his nostrils dilated with dark surmise, looked down and said, 'This boy's not in his right mind.'

"I think you must have been dreaming," she said. "I think you had visions of a child clutched between us as we trudged against a powerful dispossessing wind of darkness. The wind howled louder than your dog. In this wind, the moon knew the unsteadiness of the signaling lantern. And the tighter you held onto the child's shivering wrist, the more you seemed to be drawing the thin arms out of the body as if it were only the bucket plunged in darkness down the well that you knew would never meet your lips again.

"As we walk forward, the child slips farther and farther behind us. The child's outstretched arms are drawn into milky filaments of light. Though you squeeze tighter the puckering hand, though you can still feel the curving fishback of life in your palm and despite the fact that you are finally confident of overtaking this wind with your hurrying stride the child has disappeared between us. The child's arms have pulled out into long, whipping kite-strings broken off in the distance where invisible branches hold the higher parts of the world out of reach.

"Yet you don't let go. You can't let go because your hand is still clenched around a tiny bundle of fingers. You can count them in your mind. Do you remember how many?"

With her hands poised on her own body like tense fingers in the skin of an orange, Dinah waited for Moertle's answer.

She repeated, "Now shall I open the musical fruit?"

Her word was good. She had sung the night through. The door of her dressing room was still stiff with its thrown bolt. In the window glass, the dimming image of the room preserved an unrippling reflection of a woman throwing stones, of a man kneeling over turbulent water. She had flung her singing arms at him, thrust her dancing feet at the floor. But the walls were upright, the floor did not buckle and fall. And now, at this end of night, the sultry air of the room heavy with breathing and saturated with song and sweat, finally precipitated out the words he had been waiting for:

"Now I shall open the musical fruit."

Her hand touched her hip like a wand. And where Moertle would have counted her last rib with a pendulous finger, the gown parted. He could hear nothing from the zipper's dry mouth. But the silence was given

47

forceful tongue by the slow deliberate revelation of green ruffled corset and red garters. Her exposed thigh tops squeezed the whites of his eyes. Her knees, lifted out of the well of the discarded gown, left him on a darkened precipice. Her fingers were now prying the wings off the back of an invisible insect where they troubled the corset clasp, where the bottom of the corset thrust a jointed finger of whalebone against the soft skull of Moertle's heated consciousness and he knew a trembling membrane of silk was all that guarded the mysterious union of her legs. Moertle felt his gaze fall away from his face.

The corset popped open at the bottom. And the revealed triangle of black silk blinked full in the cowboy's naked face. Moertle looked back without blinking. In that delicately perched stillness the abrupt syncopation of Dinah's swivel hips was enough to bump him into the abyss.

But he was not falling. He was walking. His hand at his side was anticipating the bulging shape of the doorknob when out of her own empty palm, dipping at the top of the falling bodice, seizing the moment, Dinah produced a single shimmering breast—and then another out of the other hand—deftly crossing her arms over her chest, her knees kissing, her fingers squeezing with undisguised pleasure this self-created anatomy of the dawn.

Moertle now saw what he had meant to deflect with all the unflinching muscles and crackling sinew of his narrow back. The bones that poked through the expression on his face were the bones of the steer when the skin falls away from the frame in loose rubber strips. From sheaths of sequined fabric, untied ends of lace and loosened bands of silk, there was revealed before him as strange a pattern of divination as would be discovered when the animal's damp insides are turned out to dry. How could the breasts milked from her squeezing fingers ever be still again under a bib of sequined silk? Who could recapture the loosed buttocks from their wriggling distances? Who could uncoil the navel entangled in the dancing motion of her belly? The sight of Dinah bending so deeply to loosen the final black triangle from her stepping feet assured him that belly and hips were forever lost to the grip of familiar clothing, like any piece of porcelain that comes apart in both hands. Memory alone without fingers or nerves would retain its uncertain grip here no better than the hand that clutched after the vanished udder, the sawed nipples of horn, the severed tail—all irretrievably shed from ribs that had been left swinging on a silver hook for the eyes of the white-coated inspector. As though her movements were quickened by the air of the refrigeration room, her hands flying away from her breasts, her buttocks thrust away into the violet shadows, hips in a spiral, arms beckoning the blood all over her like a rash, Dinah approached on naked toes.

As Moertle passed through the door, he was not aware of the apparent deliberation with which he plucked first one agile foot and then the other out of the first coiling rays of sunlight—a silent snare—cast with lariat swiftness through the clear glass of Dinah's window.

Lilli came into the bed under a heavy drift of blankets. She had spent the darkening hours reaching into closets, and descending into trunks for more blankets to still the rattle of Moertle's bones. As the room dimmed, his face shone brighter remembering the heat that stood strong on his chest in the defeated noon. And when he protested that it was not the temperature that made his teeth chatter, she gathered the weight of her entire body to seize his trembling limbs in a stern yet reassuring grasp.

She straddled him. Beneath her lifted face, beneath the humped deformity of the covers Moertle held her hips, breasts, buttocks and thighs together in his open palms with the skills of the master rodeo rider. Aware that his fingers were somehow touching the smile on Lilli's face, he felt them working with no less certainty beneath the covers to smooth over the ragged joints and tattered seams of her body rupturing and tearing against the convulsive muscles of their perspiring labor. His hands were as quick as eyes sliding over the surface of things, seeking the perfection of the glass that holds the body's image by its impeccable smoothness. The warmth beneath the covers laid a soothing hand to his chattering teeth.

The movements of his hands, though cloaked in a quilted fabric, grew more and more visible in the features of Lilli's face. Their movement was raising the covers like a cape behind her. The sensation of speed she gave him urged his hands faster and faster to keep up until he caught the stiff pommel of her rhythm again, knowing that as fast as she could go she would not be separated from him by those cleaver lights of time that sever the cars of a freight train in their furious passage. With the shutterspeed of both hands, he retained the features of her face as intractably as the unblurred photograph of a speeding train. In the failing light above, Lilli's cries detonated abruptly. Her smooth brows, her red mouth, the wings of her nose were all violently pulled apart by an ecstatic contraction of the muscles that at the last moment lunged wildly from behind the bars of her face. And just as suddenly released from the wringing hand of that emotion, her features composed themselves again into a picture of mild serenity that she lowered to Moertle's lips on a kiss.

His eyes were closed.

THIS IS A WARNING

Report all stray animals. Alive or dead. Refrain from touching enigmatic carcasses. Stock animals are a source of pestilence. Each joint is a close dark hive of putrefaction that begins to buzz with life the instant the animal has ceased to twitch. The nostrils of a dead animal breathe, like the skin of a warm cheese, the first fumes of corruption that will leave far bigger holes in its thick hide. The dead tongue conceals in its prickly fat the smooth white worms of a wriggling life that not even the professional herdsman knows to ask about. The eyes are stagnant pools. *Do not* break the scummy surface. *Heed* the signal of the bloated belly. The interior organs contain septic gasses boiled up by the sun. Even as the bones of the animal stiffen, the bladders heave. The blood tubes are stretched like wet hairs across ballooning membranes. Spleen touches stomach for the first time the instant before they both explode. And *beware* the recondite fermentation of the bowels. *Stand clear* of the tail as though it were a lighted fuse. *Prevail* upon a passerby to guard the area. *Tell* all you know. *Make* him swear good faith and then *summon the proper authorities.*

Dr. Hugo Face

I cap my pen without satisfaction.

The public will not be warned. Our days are too much the same refrain. The streets are too familiar here. The air is too still. The sky is unmoved. Nothing drops out of the blue to goad our amazement. So the mirage of a dead steer kneeling in the dusty way sets people's jaws to hungrily biting the air. They gather around any new pile of bones because it reminds them of what it's like to be surprised. They stand still in the belief that miracles are tendered to those who wait without reason or purpose on an interminable, dry day.

They don't care if every carcass bears the unmistakable tattoo of the nearby slaughterhouse—horn and hoof cleft by a cleaver—because no one can point to a hole in the walls of the bleeding establishment to show us how the animal leaked out. Our people prefer the question unanswered, incubating in the golden belly of a dust cloud kicked up with their own restless feet on an abandoned street that should have been closed by the authorities, or behind the stage of an empty opera house where the doors are left open, or even on a busy sidewalk where we meet every day, not three steps from the sweating fire hydrant. Here the head of the steer falls (from its last step) at our feet, swollen as though with the mouthful of weeds, the tongue of water that would have saved it, would have held it upright on a green field against a spotless sky.

Each dying animal comes to us after wandering the perimeter of our city streets like a weary wheel. There is nothing beyond it. I imagine them wading tentatively out into the distance beyond and the harsh, dry unplanted distances washing them back in, on wave after wave of daily drought. So back they must lumber with their hooves split and their sides caved in like the wall of an old prairie sod house. By then the disease is already marked like a patch of poisoned grass on their tongues. The germ-swelled lips tremble with the warning they can never speak, as these empty carriers step silently back into our midst. Falling under the laundry line in a brightly manicured back yard, under the shredded striped awning of an abandoned grocery, on the tracks where the first train of the day is due, beside a parked car without udders or tail—in these thickening shadows the follicles of disease are sprouting the beard that will at last disguise us to ourselves.

My Moertle stirs in the breeze of 150 switching tails. He forces them through a single opening in the wide corral so they might pass more easily into the main building beyond. The main building waits at the end of a long narrow corridor of fencework. A bigger mouth will devour them there. When my Moertle has squeezed the last one into the narrow path, he touches his wand to a pumpkin-colored haunch and watches them begin the slow peristaltic movement of their fat march to the slaughter. He waves the electric prod, like a divining rod over the ground as he goes behind the herd.

When his eyes stop switching back and forth over the rump of the last cow, touching both walls of the corridor with his swinging gaze, you can see the trap already springing shut in his mind. He does not even break step. His hand goes out in the most erstwhile handshake. But it seizes the steer's tail like a length of the hangman's rope. He is already pulling it before the hooves realize the ground has stopped moving beneath them. He sets his feet like stakes in the ground. Hauling the steer toward him with one hand, leaping ahead until he can tuck the prod into a fold of the animal's long perspiring throat, then swinging himself all the way around the front of the animal and, in the arc of that movement, pushing the horns out of his face, he throws his back against the fence. It yields like a swinging door under the doorman's white glove. And when the steer turns sideways to follow him on slow eyes, my Moertle is already crouching in front of it again, blocking the corridor, the electric prod buzzing no bigger than a horsefly but hot as a rick of burning hay. The steer swings its weary head out of the orbit of the fly to find itself somehow slipped from the noose of white fencework that was leading it. With head and shoulders stuck perilously out into the wide plain, its nose dripping on the open horizon, it bellows its confusion.

But it will not long consider the lolling tongue of flatland, the unherded distances, when it feels my Moertle stuffing its rump with the burning hay.

The open length of fencework swings to, locked with the key of invisibility, smooth as the white of any searching eye. My Moertle holds the secret sesame in his fingertips. Arms crossed, hands on biceps, patting the smug muscle of exertion, my Moertle contemplates with satisfaction the miracle of the steer on the other side of the whitewashed fence.

Then he shoots a finger at the spotted dog sitting on his heel. The dog comes to life with the movements of all bullet-stricken animals. But its bark is the discharge that carries the steer away.

MONOLOGUE OF THE SPOTTED DOG

The master's hand flaps out on the breeze. Shaky finger. The command is stuck in his mouth fat as a beef heart. I let out from between my jaws everything that

54

sticks in the narrow passages of this scrawny man's frightened life.

I blew that animal off its hooves like the flame off a candle. Lucky for him. Lucky for a scrawny man who has to fly his own face around his head just to keep the other eyes off him. They would stick to his face like flies to fresh blood if they could see what he was doing here. But all that's left to be seen he holds between his patting hands and cuddles to his face. I'll be his beard.

"Kiss."

The doctor's black case made small clicking noises beside Moertle's panting chest. His body stretched the length of the mahogany bed, touching hollow wood at both ends.

Lilli's face floated anxiously on the perimeter of the bed. Her buoyant movements supplied the incongruous grace of the swan's back to the doctor's quacking consultations. From the opposite doorway, the chirping presence of children poked through an eyelet of the old woman's shoe. They did not know what to do. They knew the doctor pronounced life and death with a special emphasis. They told each other, here was one who had been shaken down a beanstalk, slender as the tornado dangling on the horizon. He had eaten Englishmen. They had never seen a man so fat.

"The body is all here," the doctor finally spoke directly into Lilli's face, "but I can't tell you exactly where the mind stands."

He passed a hand before Moertle's unblinking eyes. Lilli flinched. Among the children standing in the doorway the girl named Myrtle felt the other bodies pressing more insistently behind her.

"But plenty of boys have been stuck right through by the sun. They just pulled it out of the wound like a hostile arrow and went on. They came out of it as easy as stepping out of their front door; or maybe they just hear the door slamming behind them for the rest of their lives, a little funny for that . . ." Dr. Face continued, distractedly snapping his fingers in the unresponding coil of Moertle's ear. The hand that was turned away from the woman's face stole beneath the covers and pinched a nipple on Moertle's chest. He blasted a knuckle into the cowboy's ribcage at close range, gouged his navel with a sharpened fingernail, ". . . but you're right he don't respond much . . ." When he turned his face back to the patient, he opened one frozen eye wide enough to examine it between steady thumb and forefinger. He made it glitter, a jeweler's rare specimen, as he brought his light closer.

Moertle was watching the boy with the udder, kneeling in a ruffled hem of green grass. The tongue stood out from his head, erect and quivering for the last drop of milk from the exhausted teat. The herd stood around him, steers and cows knee-deep in lush pastureland. Holding the last bead of milk on his stiff tongue, the boy turned his head in a perfect circle. He was licking the horizon, making it glisten like the flap of the envelope that will be carried swiftly out of the sender's hand.

As fast as he moved his head, the line of the horizon kept a steady finger moving to divide the earth from a cerulean sky. He had run to the top of the hill. The boy had buried yellow silos and jutting black rooftops under

56

the horizon, shoved them out of sight with his kicking foot, leaving nothing vertical to blur the eyeball in its steady orbit. Everything held together in the gravitational pull of intense watchfulness.

Still holding the eye on the gentle pads of his fingers, the doctor visibly shuddered to see the melting surface break, a string of pearls cascading along the length of his thumb, crossing his lifeline like three small stones across a running creek.

The boy stood within the herd now, blinded to the horizon by bumping haunch and bowing head. His bare feet stamped the same ground that was broken all around him where the animal herd clamped down on the land, knotted together. The boy didn't believe in the hand dexterous enough to loosen them from this entanglement with the prairie sod. That was why when he saw the first rider pop up on the horizon he stepped instinctively closer to a panting hide, as if he would be the tail sucked between the stiffening legs.

Now, though he could not see them, he could hear the riders circling the herd. Letting out high-pitched cries like small featherless birds, they filled the air with commotion. As though imagining the mainspring wound tightest at the moment of release, the herd moved in concentric circles toward its silent retreating center. In the smoking center of the herd, the boy rose, like something uncorked from the genie's bottle, just to keep his feet out from under the cudgeling hooves. His eyes glanced off the humped backs, were lost in an abrupt upheaval of shadow. The loud tongue of the stampede suddenly thickened in his ear. He was embraced on convulsive flanks of the herd—an ambiguous caress—forced to kiss the uplifted snout of darkness.

The ground reached his cheek with a rancorous wallop and over his head the hooves fell like stones that never land because they fall on water. The boy felt his whole body rocked by waves that crested on the fullness of his belly and broke beyond the furthest reach of his own arm on his body's length. In the cradle of this motion, his eyes clearly focused the shapes of some cows jumping over the moon. He didn't flinch from the rising or falling weight of impacted grassland flipping the sky off its back. He was splayed out like the boy with a horn-sharp hoof already rooted between his lungs. But there he rested and was undisturbed by the thundercloud storming the long grasses.

When the cloud was dissipated with all its yellow grains sowed back to the earth, the boy appeared like a miraculous crop on the land. He was spotted by the last rider whose voice still carried on the abandoned hillside. The one who had touched the boy's ear from the perimeter of the herd now reached down to squeeze his hand, flushed with the amazement of one who reaching to drink discovers that the face in the well is not his buoyant own. The child's eyes filled the deep hoofprint of this stampede like the puddles lighting human footsteps after rain.

"Alive," breathed Lifesize the range rider, looking down, drawing his horse's head out of the boy's deep scent. Lifesize had to step backward, give room to his credulity in order to watch the boy try and mount himself on the shivered legs, try to demonstrate the movement of his arms, the chalk dust of pulverized joints somehow still hinged to the brain, the brain alerted in the paste of its concussion still snapping the eyes open and closed, the whole body nerved and boned with a life that could not possibly have escaped the grindstone turn of the herd.

Lifesize, the range rider, pushed his Stetson back over a blanched brow and squinted disbelief, "How'd you do it, boy?"

Plucking a few blades of grass out of the joints in his clothing, the boy moved his mouth to answer.

"I'm ok, doc," Moertle plucked his eye out of the examining fingers. It went back into his face like a plug that lights up the whole wall. Lilli's face took some of that light seeing Moertle come so brightly back to life. But Dr. Face pushed his lips together in an expression of doubt. He couldn't have pressed harder with his foot on an earthen mound. His face began to swing from side to side like a windy lantern on a darkened hill.

The girl named Myrtle had already given herself eight steps into the bedroom. For every ten seconds that the doctor and her mother left their backs to the door, Myrtle gave herself another two steps. She traveled in a line of sight that, from Moertle's point of view, was blocked by the doctor's bulky consultation. So Moertle started when, as though from somewhere within the doctor's deep belly, Myrtle let her voice escape.

"Papa?"

Not until this moment had Moertle himself recognized the maternal longings of the doctor's stomach reaching out over the stiff reproof of his belt. The belt had as wide and as sharp a bite as the barber's strop.

Moertle's laughter broke the surface tension in the

room like a fish boding good waters. Lilli didn't hesitate but seized his hand below the covers and passed it over her lips grateful for the sound of his voice, wishing to dispel the air of the sickroom with her own sweet breath.

But the doctor wasn't smiling. And as though he had pulled her out of his own bulging back pocket, he was now holding the girlchild off her feet in front of him, restraining her from the laughing bedside. The doctor thrust one finger out. Though he pointed it directly at Moertle, it was not nearly swollen enough to stopper the mouth of rollicking pleasure.

"He ain't cured so quickly as that. Don't let him think so." The doctor was holding Myrtle off her feet but moving toward the bed as he spoke.

"You walk out of this bed and I wash my hands of the whole story. There's a germ here that's still wagging its tail at the both of us and I ain't studied it to either of our satisfaction."

The doctor wasn't even thinking anymore of the child he proffered on his belly as he pushed closer to the bed.

But now Moertle's finger was parrying the doctor's. And his face was rolled inside out with laughter, forcing the bed to make shrill whimpering noises against the wall.

The girlchild struck the bed with the force of the doctor's final words. He spoke oblivious to the glandular unconscious of his heaving stomach that had given this wayward daughter the motion he denied to her dangling feet. "You are laughing at yourself to think I'll ever help you back on your feet again if you get up out of this bed on them now."

But Moertle was already standing, receiving the child

off the doctor's belly. The laughter in Moertle's arms would have rocked the child to sleep if the darkness in which she dissolved was not the struggling shadow of two dense-bodied men.

So Moertle handed the child into her mother's arms. He took the doctor's shoulders affectionately in his two hands and touched the forehead in between with his lips. He wiped his mouth. He stepped away from the trembling belly. He did not staunch the laughter. He could not.

So he unceremoniously clothed his own nakedness in front of wife, children and family physician and departed. There were tears in the corners of his eyes, wrung out by the muscles of hilarity. The wriggling fingers of the joke stayed buried in his gut until the last shadows of the street fell away from his shoulders and he stood shivering before his own door.

My papa lives in a house apart. I will take 365 steps before I reach it from the foot of my mother's bed. I know my steps are right because I allow for the changes in my growing foot. I keep a close watch.

When I step up to my papa's door, I will hear he has already started the conversation that he will let me take up like litter from his floor. He has no ears for my feet. He has already begun to lard his little dog's ears with soft finger-gouts of description, the colors of his boyhood whipped up into stiff curds of emotion on the back of his telling tongue. When he speaks of colors and shapes, his fingers are moving eagerly over the dog's ears as though these were his most perfect brushstrokes. In the pauses he

cleans the spittle from his moustache. Then, dipping the
bristles of his moustache into speech again, my papa tells
me how to see it.

"You must look into the streets of our hometown with
the deep staring eye of the lizard. Its scales are older than
the shingles that fall from the oldest house on the land,
where it lies under a rock that has never been kicked.
When the lizard spits its tongue into the street, it is forked to signify the two paths of our minds that from the
moment of their first divergence will never meet again."
My papa says past and present make a man stand back to
back with himself.

"But though its tongue is forked, the lizard's brain,
sealed in a green carapace of baked slime, hard as a seed
crushed under the weight of a pharoah's tomb, belongs
irretrievably to the past.

"The lizard lives longer than the man. The lizard lives
175 years. Under the beaded surface of its eye, a single
grain of life swells like dust inside a globule of water to
which the years add surface tension like drops from a
dropper. So when the man's eye is tearfully drained off
into the reaches of his shattered and dessicated home, the
eye of the lizard swells with its sweet vista of swaying
grassland watered from its own natural spring of memory. The man sees only how the grass has been razed off
the prairie lands, roofs blown away, walls caved in, debris
ingested through the narrow streets by the violent and
painfully indrawn breath of a dying town. The lizard's
vision, ripe with the quenching years, bobbles with a
crowd of lively scenes that glisten all the more brightly in
the evaporating light of time.

"The lizard's house is a hole filled with its own burrowing. But when your curiosity commands you to touch your knees to the lizard's turf and peer into those unfathomable eyes, you will only catch a glimpse of your tiny self—an image sharper and quicker than you know in the weight and density of your arms and legs—before it is clamped beneath an eyelid as severe and deliberate as the monster guillotine. I'm sure this is why they call it Gila Monster."

My papa sits on his wooden stool peering into his little dog's ear. He scrapes a ball of wax from the spiraling canal where he believes his words have tumbled to darkness.

When Papa looks at me he wishes that his eyes could be as deep as the eyes of the Gila Monster and stand as still at the bottom as he knows they must. That is what he says.

The knifeblade crescendo of the slaughterhouse turns my Moertle's voluble speech into a pantomime of glutinous chewing. He stands between two sets of swinging doors. They are misted with the freezing breath of the air compressors rumbling within. If not for the mist, he could behold the image of his oratorical self swimming freely in the mirroring depths of the door. Instead he paces between the doors. And in the sawdusted space between, he more easily turns over the fate of the animals he has led this way.

His eye follows the steel track chugging a slow train of enormous grappling hooks across the ceiling. Each hook dangles a steer at an angle to the earth that the animal never knew in life. The four legs swing together like limp rivergrass swept by a deep current. The tail hangs perfectly straight as it never did. And where the head of the creature once lifted the fattening life out of meat and bone, a muscular steel hook leads the carcass through the first set of swinging doors. When the second set of doors swings open only a man's leap away, the untempered mind of steel stands brashly revealed in the livid path of the cleaver.

No longer legs, hooves, no longer speckled hide, no longer horns, no tail to pull; but instead the chopped and peeled carcass licked by the light. It glimmers all over like the pink sliver of inner lip drawn out by a passionate kiss. As my Moertle can plainly see, the kiss of the cleaver goes as deep as the bone.

And as though a man could rise from that violet depth, my Moertle must lift his eyes to follow the progress of the herd. They are ascending along the gleaming aluminum track—one blood-plucked fruit after another—to a level far above him. They are miraculously winged with this distance—separating my Moertle forever from a haunch that first flew off his own fingertips. And where the carcasses flutter in that dimness of the vaulted roof like an overturned trough of filthy water, other hands reach out from the mezzanine catwalks to drag the heavy catch off their hooks. Because they have fished this depth for a lifetime, they are men who do not even look down anymore to reflect upon what is below them.

If they looked they would see my Moertle and have cause to wonder what monstrous form of life could be struggling to pry itself loose from his tight lips, or what shape of a hook lodged in his throat could be bent back against its intended purpose by the strength of a normal man's tongue. Because they do not see, they cannot hear his words that are absorbed into the din of resonant metal walls like the violet trace of poison annulled in the darkness of the belly deep as a sink.

"Everything preserved in mind is rendered unstable. That's what I know. And only what is lost irretrievably is preserved in its state of perfection. That's what I fear."

My Moertle the philosopher fills his words with gusts of hot breath, letting the intonation rise unnaturally as he speaks. He shakes his fist in the empty depth of the ceiling, the silent clapper of an ancient discarded bell of alarm.

"But what is the fate of the one who loses consciousness? It is surely no better to let the head float away on a wavelet of dark drowsiness than to suffer the axe— gripped high above a dilating pupil—severing the head from shivering shoulders. Who will say in what direction the head may roll?

"Yet the man who keeps his head, the man whose vocation is memory, is the warehouseman lost in the piled perspective of his own ceaseless labor. The enormous roof of the warehouse leaps higher and higher over the mounting storage. The shoulder the warehouseman throws against the shifting piles falls further and further away from the enclosing, echoing walls. The man who keeps his head keeps a tally sheet that he can never be sure of. He itemizes the failure of his own powers of observation, the tongue paralyzed in the middle of a count that will never end, that will never be verified, the ears ringing with sounds that combine as the notes of an old bell cleaving to the massive flank of still air until their resonance is no longer a movement through space but a duration as thick as the stifling air itself.

"The man who keeps his head keeps a ravenous secret. It makes the hair fall from the top of the skull. The eyes sink from view like stones in rising dough. The razor-sharp chin and the nose are all that cleave to the light until the face is as gnarled and bony as a clenched fist."

My Moertle the philosopher bows his head when it is emptied of speech. But there is something stirring yet within the empty nest of his thoughts. Because he unfolds his arms from his chest. He walks deliberately toward the perspiring wall. Refrigerator smoke pours forth like shavings of soft wood, curling from the blade of light, brandished through the murmuring double doors. My Moertle steps up to the doors. Puts his eye to the light. Forcing the soft dilated belly of the pupil against the glinting blade of light, my Moertle experiences the razor-sharp insight of the gutted eyeball. It is as though the vision that holds him to this moment has slipped from beneath the albuminous lens of his own eye to float before him, dangling eerily on this coiling umbilical line of sight.

Whether or not the butchering process is completed, he cannot tell from what he views between the doors. The cleavers are lifted still in the butchers' hands. Their white smocks are embarrassed with blood. The long trough that is also a cutting board flushes continuously into a gurgling drain. But the two butchers' faces are turned away from my Moertle's scouring eye.

Eye upon eye, nose upon nose, mouth upon mouth, my Moertle thinks they might be feeding on one another's trembling flesh to be caught in such a violent embrace. With blades raised behind one another's back, they stand as executioners before the block. Yet the arms reach up and around the meekly exposed necks only to clasp hands on the other side. My Moertle can see that under the white coats the buttocks are alive with the tense bumping motion of closely penned stock. And when they remove their mouths from one another's upturned faces, my Moertle hears the unmistakable wet breathy expulsion of the herd in its moment of stirring.

My Moertle says, "Ah!"

The two deputies Nifty and Lifesize were the first to show me yellow hands. They noticed the color one morning when they shook. And with those hands they grasped the slithering tail of an elusive pattern. Waves of perspiration troubled both their brows with a tidal regularity, and both their stomachs swayed to its sickening rhythm. Both said their joints seemed to fill with air. Their bones ached because they did not stretch. The soles of their feet cracked in their boots. They walked with legs far apart.

The two deputies sitting close together as twins on my examining table talked about their symptoms without breathing, and furiously pointed at each other to make their speech flow more smoothly. The more they talked, the more convinced I was their tongues had yellowed too.

But I was not taken entirely off my guard. The record will credit my prognostic vigilance. The blanched page of my recording pad will testify that I had already noted all the slow accumulation of sinister clues before they ever reached the tongues of these two ailing men. In the corrals I had seen: an unusually fissured hoof, a tumorous distortion of the joint crowning the hoof, the yellow tongue as large as an overripe melon, the belly inflated with the gas of the rotten melon.

Nothing conclusive. But these were the first murmurings that gained volume in the salty mouths of the two deputies. For the first time in their lives what they had to say would touch the lives of other people like a hot finger.

Of course, all my black books refuse to believe it. The print stands firm on the watery vellum and leads me the same steps over and over again to the shores of certainty: hoof and mouth is a disease of four-legged creatures. The man only sickens at the thought of losing his entire stock. The animal dies.

So I examined the upturned palms of the two deputies. I asked these boys if they'd been eating grass. I asked them if they'd been dancing barefoot on seashells to make their feet as scaly as a curving fish back. They don't say anything anymore.

Only their eyes are bigger now than they ever were, dilated with the immensity of the question their thoughts range out upon. And when I look into their eyes—open windows beckon to me—for the signs of the approaching storm, I can see farther than you can see.

The lives of animals have always held the attention of men. A man pats his dog's back to feel the hair shed from his own palm. So this is how I explain the two metal bed frames trembling against the cement floor of my wardroom. The sheriff's best men lie like man and wife, one beside the other. And when the clatter of the beds against the floor subsides, when the fever breaks, then hands go

68

out over the empty space that divides them. Because they must hold between them the heart of this thing, beating its invisible body to death like someone killing a bird with a stick.

Because the mind can tell the body a few things that it never knew by feeling. Because now I am ready to publish my hypothesis: these two men suffer from an affliction of the mind, not the body. They stood too long in the shadow of the dead steer. Though it didn't leave any mark on the surface of their bodies, it must have been cast through them like a net through water, dredging the life that hovers at the depths. Because hoof and mouth is a disease of four-legged creatures. A man with the symptoms must have only put them on like mourning clothes to show his heart. A cow's heart is the size of a man's brain. So there is something between them—a reason to believe that one could fall under the influence of the other like its own quaking shadow. Hoof and mouth is a disease of four-legged creatures.

And yet suppose a man falls from his own bodily weakness. If he has leapt from the flaming tower of his fever, and landed on all fours, or, rising from his sickly faint, attains only to his watery knees, his hands steadying his body such a short distance above the wobbly ground, if he lets his aching head graze limply between humped shoulders and feels his hindquarters tense against the pull of his head—is this sufficient likeness to the beast he drives ahead of him to drag the weary herdsman into the deepening tracks of the disease? Did these boys, who are sweating in my beds like a fatty rind spitting from a skillet, let their minds wander too closely to the hide they touched but could not feel for? If they had never thought about the way the animal suffers to its death, would these boys be walking on their two good feet apiece instead of watching them ripen at the foot of the trembling bed? Propped on pillows at the opposite ends from their own heads, do their swollen feet peeping out from the covers appear as other heads with thoughts of their own? And is that the truth: that they are swollen with thoughts the mind won't contemplate?

Though it makes a mockery of all my well-charted knowledge of the body's secret distances, I am bound to ask such questions.

Up the road, my Moertle walks toward the place where he was born. The stone-lined hole is the gutted foundation of his childhood home. In it he still sees the swirl of ashes, the black devouring tongue of smoke that leapt up to catch his father and mother like flies off the flaming wall before plunging into a silence thick and tarry as the pits that swallowed reptiles whole in the ancient deserts. He can still blacken his hands on the foundation stones lying loosely like potatoes that have never been plucked from the coals. My Moertle observes that the grassland fluffed out around his house like folds of a woman's long gown—finding a place for herself on the sloping ground—was ravished to the roots.

It is as though the dissatisfied fire had stalked out of the falling frame of the house and paced its frustrations out from one end to the other of the vast surrounding plain, scorching everything in sight. But my Moertle knows it was only the trod of heavy years of drought that wore this dusty path through the world of his childhood.

My Moertle strikes the tip of his boot against the dead flint of scorched foundation stones. Only a few fluttering wings of dust alight from this contact. Lifting his eye to that height where the roof once squinted against his own luminous bedroom window, my Moertle's eye meets the burning gaze of noon. He coolly places his eye against the sun as one puts a finger to the candle's flame, to test the strength of his vision. Because my Moertle claims he can still see the roof of the house peaked against the hanging sky. He claims his eye still bulges with the angles of four walls, the stone weight of bricks and mortar. His eye hangs upon the world with the density of objects that have ceased to exist for the ordinary man. He says the tear ducts of his eyes—not for mourning—irrigate his view of prairie land with the memory of long grass combed by a mild wind, the herds nestled in the grass like painted eggs. Pink birds arise from their secret nests.

Yes, the remarkable thing is my Moertle's ability to apply his lips to the past, to gather his lips around familiar words and to suckle the life of them as it flows into his arms of gesticulating speech.

"Here was the heaving blue breast of a pond where the cattle found their faces like huge sunken stones in its cool depth. And there was the trough of corn, belly up in the throbbing sunlight. Here was a stand of leaning trees. Their shadows flooded the grass with the smell of dampness that was clutched at their roots. And there was a road. It flowed all the way back to the white house, lifting over the softest rise like the glittery fish back struggling upstream onto fertile shoals."

Even with his gaze stuck through by the shaft of the sun's ray, my Moertle tells it all.

71

My Moertle stooped so lowly in the waving grass he would not have been seen by anyone passing a shrunken eye over the sunlit land. But my Moertle's own gaze grew immense in the thickest part of pasture greenery where he once crouched, holding the slim tail of a snake out of its throttling hole. The green head of the snake buried itself like a pea in its furrow. My Moertle neither pulled nor allowed his grip to be broken. He calmly held the slick tail, thrilled by the violent telepathy of the burrowing head. Because his own eyes jostled in the hole with the squirming length of the snake, he didn't see thin arms leaping out of the grass by his heels to seize his ankles. His feet were pulled against the blue sky as if he had kicked off a cloud. His mouth closed hard upon the hole where the snake had leapt. He no longer had knees to hold him to the ground; but he was splayed upon it and his back could feel the bursting cocoon of little Lilli's crawling weight.

She was already on top of him. She rode him, her own back lifted into the air like a roused snake, her laughter showering over my Moertle's bowed head like the roar of an arena. So, he put down his head even lower, threw his straddled haunch into the air, began his own bucking rodeo dance. With the girl's bare feet tucked like spurs under his belly, her wet hands ripping the collar of his shirt, he reverberated his bellowing snorts against the shivering walls of her laughter. Lilli rose above the grass and fell as erratically as a bee in clover. With hammering knees, my Moertle crushed the clover to a pulp. But when the shirt rode far up on my Moertle's back and he felt the hot breaths of her bumping behind, he turned— like someone who, touched from within by the body's own reflex, nonetheless reaches for the innocent face beside him.

What my Moertle saw behind him as he turned held him in two enormous hands of tranquility. Hands cupped for ladling mouthfuls of glassy water. He rolled over onto the sky as it drew its darkening blanket over the far end of pasture. But it was the grass he felt beneath him. It was the tiny waist of the girl he felt beneath him, brittle as a bright pinky ring lost in the grass beneath him, as he turned to watch the blackening clouds mount on puffy knees gathering strength, suffused with the already bruised blood of impending storm. My Moertle did not notice the tiny fists that were falling like stones into the hot dough of his stomach. He mistook the struggling movements of the girl who now lay beneath him, as though he had collapsed on his own shadow, for the effects of the weather, which had by now planted heavy feet on the ground and begun to dance on the taut drumhead of pastureland.

My Moertle lay in Lilli's most violent embrace as the rain fell faster and made him slick in her arms. Lilli's slick arms were a dangerous cradle for my Moertle's rocking motion. She was swallowing rainwater, she was swimming beneath him and as the piled weight of the sky began to collapse in ragged blocks of stone, she was frightened to feel the thundering noise reverberate from inside my Moertle's belly. For my Moertle was forcing his lips to carry the sound of crumbling firmament and he strained with the effort of a slave bent beneath a burnished block of sandstone. But only little Lilli clutched at his back and now she was hanging on even as he struggled to rise.

Lilli thought he rose with the buoyancy of all the air that must have filled him up, for he expelled it then. With his knees steady on the earth again and his mouth turned upward, he gave up to the full dome of the sky the spreading wings of his voice. Like a pebble down a dry well-shaft it sounded the high-pitched shriek that only the small ears of an inexperienced boy would mistake for the resounding clap of a thunderhead. Though he stood up at last and heaved his chest into the wind for ballast, though he opened his mouth wide enough to expel an iron ingot, Lilli heard only the solitary plucked string of a child's thin voice.

My Moertle heard only his thunderous self and took it as confirmation when, lowering his gaze to breathe, he saw the entire cattle herd assembled on a pasturey rise before him. Assembled and moving. The thunder that rang from beneath their hooves, he thought, was the perfect echo of his own panting lungs. Though it came up from the ground into their trembling legs, little Lilli believed it might have fallen from the air. Standing, shaking at the bottom of the hillock, both of them felt the danger drawing closer, the water rising between their toes, the wind smothering them between its enormous breasts, the herd coming through the rain like clarity hurled through a fogged windshield.

Lilli's little hand was burrowing into my Moertle's tight fist. But he would not take cover. Even with the sky falling all about them, my Moertle's head remained erect in the knowledge that everything flows together in a turbulent stream. In the coiling eye of the storm, the venom of time's serpentine movement is neutralized. Where the

74

currents swarm like clouds of flies around a speck of meat, a calm descends: there where the shiny tip of the screw bites most peacefully into the wood, there, nothing will alter.

Screwed to the earth, though it bucked and buffeted him, my Moertle praised the enflamed temper of the sky. My Moertle exclaimed upon the aura of the watered grass, sang the eloquence of thunder, cheered the unanimity of the elements. Pressing each word into Lilli's ear as tightly as wads of protective cotton, he begged her to stand firm. He ordered her to make her legs stop dancing the dance of the puppet with tangled strings. She hung limply in his laboring arms. He pulled her up and let her down as he spoke in more and more frenzied rhythms, pacing the rapid approach of the herd with breathless words. Though the matronly apron of the enormous, white clapboard house billowed in the windy distance behind their backs, my Moertle forced Lilli's shoulders in line with the horizon that was before them: brown and moving. And when the herd was close enough that my Moertle's nostrils twitched with the dusty pollination of a hundred churning hooves, he pressed his mouth to Lilli's ear—as though he must speak through a quivering length of rubber tubing—and disgorged the last indigestible flower of his speech:

> Fie, fie, my dear,
> We are children who never grow old.
> The spell is already upon us,
> As our shadows flee from the road.

And when he looked up again, the hundred lowered heads and horns presented eyes as well.

I track my Papa onto the road that carries him home to easy arms and a rocking motion that I love too, though he never carried me home. But in my mother's house and on my own, if I push the blankets up against the closet wall until it cradles my curving back, I can rock myself to sleep and catch my Papa where he crouches under a purple stone.

But for now I just follow him down the road unobstructed by rocks or clumps of grass big enough to make a hiding place. Only the sun falls on my Papa's shallow footsteps. And though it leaps like a bandit and wrings my neck with its dusty hands, it is no obstacle to me; because my Papa taught me to balance a bubbly oasis of mouth water on the back of my tongue and to walk for miles over a baking crust like the veiled woman of the Nile carrying a cool earthen jug on the top of her head. My Papa doesn't see the feat of my balancing act. He mistakes my careful footfall behind him for the hail of small pebbles kicked up by his own rapid, careless step. I am the eyes in the back of my Papa's head. But what I see I see by burrowing in.

As he walks, my Papa's head wags from side to side as though he were coming up behind the herd with his switch. And he is just as certain about where he is going as he would be turning in the stock corrals. The road is winding and coiling tightly into the distance. But my Papa turns with each movement of the road as naturally as though he is threading the flanks of the herd through the needle's eye opening in the fencework of the corral.

But when he finally stands before the brick-lined foundation hole cradling the word home on its blistered lip, I can see that the steadiness of his bearing when he walked upon the road has bolted—the one small dogie that can startle the whole herd over a cliff. Because my Papa has already begun to talk. His mouth is already moving like the wings of a butterfly caught in a sticky web.

First, he blows on his lips. It sounds like he is snorting into a trough of water. It even wets his lips and makes the word "Papa" spring off his tongue like the slippery fish. "Mama" gushes after. And right away, holding his head against an invisible beam, pushing up from the lower half of his body, he is suddenly standing beneath the triple-storied, clapboard-shuttered column of thin air and carrying its whole weight on one stooped shoulder. Slowly descending into a squat, he must let it all down with greatest aplomb, careful to remove his toes before it touches ground. Now everything is in place. From the bottom of this teetering squat, his eyes rise to a small bump on the horizon. He has not stopped talking—"We are children who never grow old"—but his eye does not move off its target. And he doesn't need to stand up to see because the only barrier to the horizon on this flat land has so long ago been swallowed into the hole at his feet.

So it is while my Papa makes a frog of himself on this scalded lily pad of space that I begin to understand the convulsions of the tadpole coming into his new life. I have held the tadpole like a moving eye in the palm of my hand.

My Papa's eye doesn't move. But the rest of him begins to unravel from the tight knot of his gaze until he is actually sprawled before the open pit. And though his eye has

77

now fallen from the horizon too, the complexity of the knot has absorbed him like water, which makes it impossible for even the nimblest fingers to untie it. And while it looks like he is fallen from a dangerous height, I can see his body is still moving rhythmically on the ground.

The closer I get, the smaller my Papa seems to me, as if I remain on the cliff he fell from. But the ground under my feet doesn't even rise above the tracks I make in it and my Papa is not twitching from the prod of any guileful hand that I can see.

Now his eyes are shut and he is flat to the ground. Anyone would think, "Here is a man struck hard by the sun," and help him to a gulp of water that might float him back to the surface of life again. But after the first sip, they would think they had drowned him because the tears are already squirting out of his pressed eyelids. His arms, crossed over his chest, are struggling to keep him afloat. His entire body shudders under some vast and invisible current of air that blows over him, that I swallow with my own words and taste like dirt when it swirls above me. But this time my Papa doesn't get up like I would have seen him do any other time. He just lies there rattling against the ground, the sky pouring smoke on the horizon until the daylight is burnt out.

Now, I know that in the darkness I can creep ever closer to my Papa's side: on my hands and knees I will sound four-legged against his darkening eardrum. And I can get even closer this way, breathing slowly with my head grazing low to the ground until when I am so close that if my Papa were the last blade of grass on the prairie, I wouldn't even have to stretch out my tongue, he reaches up and snaps me to his chest.

". . . the spell is already upon us, as our shadows flee from the road . . ." These are the words from his lips though his heart has leapt even more swiftly into my ear, pounding every other sound hard against the thin walls of my hearing.

But I am not at all frightened. Because he holds me as though he is carrying me home. Because his embrace is dark and confined as a narrow closet. Because I feel the ticklish warmth of so many blankets emanate from his enfolding arms I know that had I ever rocked long enough on the closet floor at home, this is where I would have found myself when I tumbled awake.

> Lillifalura, falura lures me
> La la lo lo Lilli, the whore . . .

And then I realize that tight as his arms are gripping me, the shape that conforms to their strength is not entirely my own. Though his wrists are cinched against the small of my back, he leaves room around my waist enough to crack a pair of coconuts between his forearms and each hip. He is pressing me to his chest but we do not touch, as though it would take forever to squeeze the air out between our two bodies. Even against my belly there bulges a space that is round and warm but empty as the ringing of a bell.

But before I can put out my hand and furtively touch the swelling shape of the imaginary one who is crowded invisibly into this embrace with me, my papa thrusts his own hand into a part of myself—hot and violent as it is—that I would never have felt from within. It is as though he were to pluck with molten fingers a tiny tooth-shaped piece of ice from between my legs. Because when

79

I seize the hand and worm my finger into its clenched palm, there is only a wet chill and nothing for me to hold up to the moonlight between dripping fingers. And there is not even enough time to finish straining my sight through the sieve of moonlight before his hand recoils into his five fingers and struggles back between my legs.

I am astride his chest, pushing off from the ground on either side to escape the erratic flight of his hand. But it is so dark that I cannot be sure we are not both flying since I can no longer use my feet to distinguish the ground from the air they dangle in. Or is my Papa deliberately arching his back against the ground to confuse it with the air I breathe? And I must swallow huge draughts because he is prying my mouth open with his searching fingers, though they are far below and though I cannot expel a single sound from my quivering lips. The darkness is compacted there like an empty footprint. Now I know how much I want to cry out, to force my tongue out of its deep burrow and struggle free from Papa's unswerving hand.

So when I am able to untangle my hand from the net of frantic movements that is thrown over us both, I know instantly there is only one way to pluck myself from the night. And because my mouth is already forced open on a wedge of darkness, I need no other movement than to lift, to plunge the tips of my fingers into the bottom of my throat and cause the enormous green frog crouched in my stomach to leap. In one swift movement I have stolen the fire from my Papa's hand—though it lurches uncontrollably through all the writhing channels of my body—and calmly poured it out on his shocked face.

Though I have finally seized the mystery he clenched

within me and propelled it out into the hungry space of my own seeing, it is much too dark to see anything. Instead there is only the slow choked sound of my Papa's breathing, the slippery movements of his hands over his disfigured face, the harsh, sour smell of the green frog if it had hopped into a busy roadway.

And through it all my Papa is still speaking. His words come to me now like pieces of cheese passed under my nose:

. . . The spell is already upon us . . .

But these words are not for me. I know he will not speak to me because he is standing now, pacing nervously in one direction then another, wiping his hands on the ruffled robe of darkness, or like a man furled in yards of billowing drapery groping for a bright seam. Peering with greater intensity into the depths of these sounds, at last I can make out only myself crouching alone at the end of the long dark tunnel of my hearing, through which my Papa has obviously fled.

With a tiny gasp I find that the hand that has plucked me from the night's spinning vortex is my own and will not loosen its grip between my bending legs.

Though my Moertle waits at the furthest corral from the slaughterhouse walls, he is holding his ears against the din of bursting life echoing within. Amidst the penned and motionless herd, his head between his hands rests as gingerly as the ticking bomb that would detonate the hooves into a stampede. He is like a man who, hurrying with an open cannister of kerosene, knows nonetheless with absolute and already grieving certainty that the

81

random spark will find him before he reaches the tank. And though he cannot hear and though he cannot see through the corrugated aluminum walls of the slaughterhouse itself, he knows that the engines of butchery have ignited in their enormous steel housings. The hammers have begun to fall, raining blows through the moist darkness; the hooves of the headless beasts are already dancing in air to the music of the conveyor belt as it drags them along.

The earth gives them up to the air and the air gives them up to the fire of glistening knives. Patiently counting the seconds before he too will be called to account, my Moertle enumerates the steps of the process he understands so well.

First the axe falls against the neck like an echo of the hammer it waits upon. As the head falls away from the body but before the legs feel the abandonment of all sensation, the descending jaw of darkness has snapped up the carcass with its tooth of gleaming steel. It slowly begins to close against the roof of the building. Before the shocked eyes have blinked shut in the severed head, they will be struck with the image of the legs ascending above them. The puffy cheeks touched by sawdust below gather the last sensations of barnyard nesting, the smell of the toppled forest, the sound of the trickling brook as the blood soaks into the floor.

And up above, the emblazoned intelligence of the sparkling steel hook resolutely conducts the carcass through swinging doors, animating it with the jerky movements of another life, one unbidden by the green pasture and the blue pond but one no less rigidly instinctual in the steel track that winds its course across the ceiling toward an inexorable submission: submission first to the axe that disposes of the no-longer essential hooves and then to the long, delicately curved and serrated blade suitable for sectioning a grapefruit if it were the size of a man, but expressly designed to shiver the hide loose from the corpulent flesh. The tail drops to the floor like the hangman's last bit of rope. And the carcass ascends higher amidst the lamentations of chain and pulley.

But before the carcass can escape the eye of the man left standing below it, my Moertle is reminded that the carcass, held aloft, ready but still untouched by the white-coated arms proffering the last and most violent embrace of the butchering process, resembles nothing so much as the bruised fruit of heaven. The foreshortened carcass, its stumps splayed stiffly out as though nailed to the wall that actually hovers thirty feet in the distance; the torn belly; the tensed, exposed hindquarters; even the bowed neck of the hook that bears its remaining weight; all awaken the image of the tiny suffering god cut out of wood in my Moertle's remembering mind.

For now, with his head thrust so far back in the darkness of his lullaby mind, my Moertle realizes that what has caught his upturned inquisitive face under the chin is the firm hand of devotion. It had reached out of a kindred darkness to his childhood self, its invisibility and its vividness enhanced then by the enormous dizzying vault of the chapel roof, and the rumor of blood running swiftly on the lips of the other communicants as they gulped out of the corners of my Moertle's eyes. Standing where he stood then ·among others much larger than himself, deriving all the support he could from the shaky wooden rail, his gaze was powerfully solicited by the brown and shriveled wooden figurine hung on the bare wall like the last bat unroused from the rafters.

Despite the more solid rail of the corral where my Moertle leans the weight of his grown-up self, his gaze remains adrift in the darkness—where at the highest reach of the vaulted ceiling he sees the bobbing fruit finally plucked from its hook, the empty bough left swinging, as a rattling of cleavers raises up before the mind's eye the forest of trees about to be felled.

With his ears tuned to the sound of catastrophe, my Moertle hovers for a moment between two darknesses. He is waiting for the whistle to blow, the voices of the other hands to echo the command back along the path to the corral as through the arched passageway of a castle or a cathedral. Then my Moertle must lift his electric prod and prick the flanks of the herd out of their dream of stillness.

Watching. Waiting. But walking too my Moertle moves to the command of the whistle. As he is feeding the last lengths of the herd into the narrow alleyway that leads from the corral to the ready mouth of the main building, he readies himself for an act that will sever him from all other hands so concerted in their effort to magnify the sounds that bellow from the slaughterhouse walls.

The black-and-white-spotted dog at his heels, my Moertle follows the last steer into the corridor of fencework where everything flows together as from a common source. His own hips fall naturally into the rhythms of the steer's brown haunch. It is the hour when the sun holds every other man's eye forcibly to the ground. But my Moertle is so completely swept along by the rhythms

84

of the steer's forward motion that he needn't pay attention to the ground in front of him, and he is free to cast his sights to the office windows staring out with such clear accusation from beneath the eaves of the slaughterhouse roof. One by one his searching eye wipes clean the likeliest spots of suspicion from the lens of public scrutiny through which he could be seen: the last turn of the wooden alleyway into the reach of long shadows lunging from the slaughterhouse entrance, the delicate iron catwalk ringing the upper stories, the crow's nest aloft of the spinning windmill where a few birds roost. He is counting his footsteps now, dropping their empty shells behind him in the dust as the hunter advancing on the carcass with his smoking gun.

Suddenly the steer's stiffening tail is a burning fuse in my Moertle's fist. Pulling back with one arm and thrusting his body forward with the same convulsive movement, he uses the prod to make the steer bow its head, and cuts in front of it. His body sails in a fluid arc across the steer's path until he strikes the exact length of fencing that he was looking for, and, as the blow is struck, lets the fence sway away from his stinging hip. As the steer lifts its horns into the shredded air, my Moertle ducks beneath it, cuts back across its bewildering path and strikes again with the electric prod, but this time between the hind legs and high up where the strong bones and heavy flanks give way to a soft, tightly squeezed bag of skin. The steer's hooves kick as high as my Moertle's teeth and leave the space of alleyway gaping wide behind it.

My Moertle tosses his hat after the brown haunch when it is irretrievably on the other side of the fence. He

85

whoops. He stamps his foot. Finally he leans over the fence, letting his head rest gently on a gust of air. His breathing is relieved and he puts one foot up on the fence rail, waiting for the steer to shrink into the distance.

And the steer is already shrinking, squeezed by the distance that bulges between the fence and the roadway almost a quarter mile off. My Moertle squints as though to help the melting glare of the bright sun soak the animal up more quickly, finish its slow evaporation, sponge the last trace of his guilty deed from the incriminating horizon.

Just when he thinks he is safe, he hears an automobile horn blow from what he took to be the steer's vanishing rump, winking like a bubble about to burst at the blurred limit of his vision. The squealing brakes confuse the image more with his mind's view of a livid mouth spreading wide with pain. And everything muddies for the moment in the increasing wetness of his concentrating eye. Silence. The cough of an engine. And the focal point of his scrutiny, small as the dilated pupil of his own eye, begins to jump. And it grows more rapidly than an explosion of thunder unfurling over the flattest tableland. Before my Moertle can jump down from the fence, the hurtling form of the steer reassembles horns, head and hooves into the very specter of doom he had been warding off with his anxious gaze. He doesn't even have time to untangle his foot from the fence rail before the entire construction is jolted like a jab from the electric prod.

My Moertle throws his hands up in front of his face, too late for the realization that he is already on his back in the dirty alleyway and too early to realize that he is in no danger from the stabbing horns because the animal

86

has caught its head between two fence boards. Before my Moertle can open his mouth in astonishment, the bellowing of the trapped steer ascends like a smoke cloud of alarm. As though the very flames were tickling his face, my Moertle reddens, snaps his head back, feels his whole face burning with the shame of discovery.

But above him, miraculously the staring windows are not aflutter with wakeful movements. He contorts his gaze over one shoulder to find that there is no excited throng streaming from the slaughterhouse gate—from the catwalks above no accusatory shriek has been flung down. Not one curious eye has popped out of the encircling landscape to draw it like a noose around him. Apparently only his own aching ears are torn with the moans of the thrashing animal.

He breathes in as though it is the last breath of air in the sky, though one more than he ever expected to take. And like someone stooping to recapture a dropped coin, he seizes the moment.

He throws down both hands as though they clutched the blanket that could smother the flames of catastrophe leaping about him. The eyes in the trapped animal's head are unflinching under the stifling blows of my Moertle's fists. The helpless horns that had somehow parted the fence boards are all that prevent the steer from escaping their grip. Then, sensing the air all around him stretched to bursting with the animal's moans, my Moertle finally feels the shock of the inevitable explosion nowhere more forcefully than in the sole of his already lifted boot as it crashes down on the slanted plane of the animal's pilloried head. The softness of the wide eyes disappears beneath the blow like the surface of water as one is crashing through into its silent depth. Though it staggers on new-born legs, the broad-shouldered steer is already heaving the bruised head into the safe distances. As though it is the arc of a single momentum that started with his foot, my Moertle swoops down to gather the only evidence of what has happened where they lie like empty powder horns at his feet. The tips of the horns have snapped clean from their mounts. In my Moertle's hands he thinks he can feel the force necessary to break bone still vibrating like the sound inside an empty shell where the mollusk once crept. Walking away from the shattered fence boards, my Moertle's chary gait is all that murmurs the accusation that he has so successfully eluded. Because where he has secreted the tips of the longhorns in the front of his denim pants, he has been discovered by an invisible hand of wrath.

"Dinah the Damsel in Distress" wept long, glistening tears. They were worked into bright trinkets by the spot-light that followed her across the stage. The crimson flow of her gown was staunched by the encircling darkness as she walked. Her voice seemed to stand upon her shoulders, loud but wavering against the balance of some wayward motion of her body. The words of the song were scintillating on the tip of her tongue, gleaming with saliva. They were turned again upon fingers of light as she reached out toward the audience, gathering the entire auditorium onto the swelling tide of her bosom. And because it must have been too much to support on the strength of her soft breast, she collapsed on the pouting lip of the stage. There, where the light washed over into a trough of darkness, she was able to rest her mourning head on a smooth upthrust shoulder of the tempestuous volcanic shore. A single weathered rock bit through the protruding lip of the stage, the only prop to suggest the windy end of land to which the song had driven her. From behind the kneeling woman, the sound of the wind rose on the tautest string of a lonely violin, the musician rocking so violently in his chair that the backdrop concealing him shook its whole forest of painted trees.

Moertle leaned over the rail of his flag-draped box to inhale the incense blowing from Dinah's loggy head. Peering down directly on top of her, he could see that the hand folded demurely into the crimson gown was actually clenched behind her back and impaled, or so it seemed, with a blazing silver baton.

> Betrug auch hier? Mein die Hälfe!
> Verräter! Ich trink' sie dir!

Peering into the hushed faces of his audience, Moertle was able to imagine that the high quavery voice singing around his head regurgitated from any other darkly mysterious throat than his own. His eyes reached out, gathering weight and substance that would clothe the hovering voice with the illusion of flesh. As he marked the features of one small girl who bounced up and down in her seat, the wooden doll acquired more solid weight on Moertle's knee. The girl's face jiggled with laughter and the balsa chest no bigger than Moertle's fist palpitated more forcefully with the life of a muscle traveling high up his arm. Because he concentrated until he was able to count the teeth in the little girl's grin, the puppet jaw clacked more audibly beside Moertle's ear. Finally, the dense body of

89

the man cracked and fell away into the shadow of the puppet's animated glee.

"Make him tell the story of the children cut from a tree!"
The semicircle of children spoke with one voice. But the ventriloquist's face was now bare of response. The carved features were as stiff as though they were still fastened by the natural grain to the inner core of the log. And the red lips of the doll were all the movement there was in response to the children's exhilarated mood.

Then the violin string snapped behind her back. As though it had been the cord that loosed the crimson gown from her shoulder, "Dinah the Damsel in Distress" stood up in a shower of light that washed every trace of blood from her skin. The note that broke from her lips might have been squeezed out by the quick fingers of brightness seizing her by the waist, sculpting what appeared to be only her malleable nudity into the silvery thorax, the sleekly trimmed waist of a stinging wasp. Caught like the insect in a jar, her body fairly buzzed within the sparkling walls of the silver leotard, arms and legs flying against an invisible obstacle until Moertle could see that the red glow catching the end of her baton was now a real flame and not the slow coal of the spider's poisonous underbelly that could be seen as one turned the jar in the light. Nonetheless the feverish movements of her legs revealed the carefully spun filaments of a bright passionate web. And the audience's eyes were caught there at the center of the stage, bulged by the curving lens of the glass jar, held by the spectacle of the invisibly clad drum majorette who now smiled the gleaming smile of the girl caught forever behind the glassy sheen of a locket photograph. From between her legs, she plucked the tongue of flame, silencing the entire hall as though she had thrust it into her own lover's mouth. She held the breath of her audience between the two nimble fingers that kept the baton turning over her head, kept the flame from licking her thighs when she thrust it between her legs again.

The wooden jaw clacked loudly enough to split a log.

"The blade of the lonely woodcutter's axe is honed to such sharpness that the wood peels away in curlicues vibrant as translucent skin. So when he finally nicks the wide cheek of the face to make a mouth for his own wooden boy, he shouldn't be surprised to see the lips so suddenly protrude, to hear the first shavings of speech curl away from what a moment before was only a dense oaken block. And what had been the cramped angles of a rough-hewn sculpture rounded into life as easily as a ball leaves your hand. The light sifted through the treetops to make the child squint and the woodcutter to hold the axe over his shoulder as though he were holding up the wall of a building that would have crushed them both. Such was his amazement to hear the child's first words:

"'Now, woodsman, free my sister from her wooden stare,' pointing to the unshaved trunk towering beside them. 'You know, she peers on nothing all day but the expanding rings of the wooden stalk. She is the pebble dropped into the still pool that is growing still all around her!'

"The good woodsman's axe then fell with the reverberating sound of tottering giants. And the axe did not cease to bite the soft wood until its owner was filled with satisfaction."

"Between the boy and the woodsman, the wooden girl at last stood on one leg, her hand extended in one direction, her face twisted stiffly in the other. Then, with the blunt head of the axe, the woodsman tipped the balance that held her to the

clearest light of this afternoon—like the sticky wings of a fly to air—and she fell alive to the gravitational forces of all the spinning world. Or whatever invisible power drew her to the earth became forever indistinguishable from the flexed net of her own physical strength that broke her fall and ever afterward carried her away on her own two legs.

"She lifted herself from all fours, to curtsy before the woodcutter's stiffening shape who now knew without a doubt that she had the roundest knees he had ever seen.

"'Kind woodsman, my limbs are as fine as your mind when you contemplated the standing tree. The thinness of my little fingernail truly measures the strength of your eye. It measures the firmness of your will, but it is also the measure of your frailty. Now I must tell you that with the sweat of your hands you have produced loss and mourning.'

"And with this, the boy and the girl joined hands across a sunstruck space of forest floor.

"And now the woodsman was on his knees begging the children not to depart. He saw in their bare, gold-hewn legs the glimmer of some darkly mined treasure of his life, flexed as those perfect legs were for a race that would brook no competitors. Then, the axe handle inverted between the woodcutter's bended knees, became a cradle against which he could rock his sorrowful head as he spoke."

And as Dinah the drum majorette drew the fiery baton one last time between her legs, a twist of her wrist inverted the flame. In the gesture of a born trooper's salute to the audience, she touched a spark to the golden hive of her hair.

And it was the explosion of the hive that stung the audience in their seats. The carefully piled hair burst with sounds of the life that is too densely impacted in the raging body of the bee.

But just as the audience felt the immobility of their seats to be intolerable, just as they thrust their feet to the floor taking wing on their worst fears, the still graceful movement of the arm that had lifted the baton began to lead the rest of the performer's body into a gentle circular motion. Poised and unhurried by the climbing tower of flames above her head, "Dinah the Damsel in Distress" began twirling. As though the still, gracefully extended arm had been the pulled string of a colorful top, she allowed her knee, her calf, and finally the foot of one leg to be swept up into the voracious swirl of hips and thighs until it was plain to see that she carried the full weight of herself on one deftly pointed toe. And as she twirled, the flame, ejaculating higher and higher above her head, appeared to be powered by the circular motion itself, until the audience understood intuitively how the two phenomena were linked, how the centrifugally elongated shape of her body sustained the spasmodic force of the flame. And as they watched the rapidly increasing motion of the body drive the flame higher into the very flies of the stage, the vertiginous fears of the audience were at last driven to fling themselves into the heat of wild applause. So, at last, by abruptly halting the cyclonic momentum of the dance, the performer could unleash the coiled rope of her hair in a crackling whip-stroke discharging the full length of burning hair, the trail of sparks, even the charred scalp to the smoking floor of the stage.

And from the very nest of the flame, the phoenix's red hair fell luxuriantly around her bowing shoulders, framing bright eyes, the milky perspiration of the white skin and all the smiling satisfaction of her face with a lurid radiance that would clearly never burn itself out. So secure in this knowledge did she appear amidst the encouraging whistles and huzzahs of the crowd that at last she raised herself from the bowing posture. She took two steps backward just to place her foot on the neck of the charred and shattered serpent that had sprung from her own head. With her conqueror's arms lifted above her, raising the level of applause all around, "Dinah the Damsel in Distress" commanded the curtain to fall at her feet.

"'*You too shall one day be old enough to beg the pity of children,' cried the woodcutter on his knees.*

"'*You too shall attain an age of regret, noticing for the first time and of course too late, that the path you have chosen bears the imprint of no other footsteps. Searching over your shoulder for the clues you mistook in your haste, you will be blinded by the light that casts only your own shadow haplessly underfoot. And then in your loneliness you will know that you must finally stop. You must shed your familiar ways. You must quietly sink into yourself and let such shapes emerge as have been hidden by the desires stretching the face over the bones in the various expressions of youthful will. And did I not act just so? Did I not humble myself to the labors of the axe? Did I not bow to the inner man whose own humility is boundless? And is this my reward?'*

"*The two children hovering in the pink aura of their nudity stood on tiptoe in the forested way. For the first time, the little girl looked at her brother with doubt, a budding tear in her eye. But her brother was unmoved and danced a few steps of an impatient jig.*

"*Pressed to the weathered grain of the axe handle, the ravaged woodcutter's face ceased to sway, though his hands held fast to the long shaft, and with the implement of his trade still*

94

planted between his bended knees, he gave the appearance of a man tied to the stake.

"But before the old man could renew the rhythms of his plea, the dance wriggling through the little boy's body like an invading worm aroused its own accompaniment in the shrill and sinuous melody that issued from his lips. Only the illusion of invisible strings plucking this music from the child's spasmodic movement caused the woodcutter to wait upon the words of the song:

> *And now that I must speak with the tongue of the tale*
> *That's been told many times and again.*
>
> *To be born from a tree is so unnaturally hard*
> *That it stretches the measure of men.*
>
> *That's the reason we move without muscle or bone*
> *In a skin that's not really our own.*
>
> *And the children of wood, though they wish*
> *That they could,*
> *Can never be cherished at home.*

"The tear ripening in the little girl's eye ran to the corner of her mouth and was swallowed in her effort to speak. She wanted to kiss the woodcutter's nodding grey head, to tell how she regretted his sorrow. She wished to pass the words old father *in a furtive glance, to see him grasp them in the furrowed skin of his brow. She even felt an urge to express her mounting fear that the woodcutter's words, where they stuck in her hearing, were tipped with invisible poison droplets of truth. But she couldn't pronounce a single word before her brother plugged all their ears with the finale of his song:*

95

Fie, fie, my dear,
We are children who never grow old,

The spell is already upon us
As our shadows flee from the road.

"*And with that the boy, who was not big enough even to touch the lowest branches of the trees, seemed to reach down from precisely that height to pluck his sister from the ground and, in the darkling palm of some magician's sleight-of-hand, to make both of them disappear.*"

As though in some eloquent testimonial to the woodcutter's speechless amazement, the words ceased to flow from the wooden lips of the ventriloquist's doll, leaving only the clacking sound of two wooden shoes ebbing away on a tide of deserted cobblestones.

Surely as I can speak I spied the man from my windy perch. Casting my leisure eye out on a sea of brown backs, skimming the daily tide of the herd that moves from the corrals to the processing plant, and being so caught up with the play of glittering surfaces, I little expected anything to break from the depths of that somnolent routine. At first, to relax and to enjoy the special solitude of the windmill tower were my only desires. But presently, as the calm of the roaring blades descended like some enormous deafening headgear, I began to let it weigh against the problem lodging uncomfortably in my consciousness. I used it to build leverage against this problem until I might shift it like a stone from the mouth of an enchanted cavern.

One of the hands was dead. One of the beds in my

infirmary had ceased to accompany the rattling frame of its fever-racked neighbor. We had already stripped the bedclothes from the mattress.

Yet, if I didn't miss my guess, this bed wouldn't be empty for long. Contagion is something I know about. And when contagion casts its wide net from the white plateau of the sickbed, somebody gets caught. From where I stood aloft of the tottering windmill, I suspected that I might be the first to see what would be dredged up onto the golden shoals of a fine summer's day. So, despite the reproachful words of medical dicta—"Hoof and mouth is a disease of four-legged creatures"—I maintained my vigilance.

So it was no longer with a casual eye that I noted the calculated indirection, not to mention the undeniable two-leggedness, of a human figure nosing its way through the intricate mazework of the corral below. First he moved with his front and then he moved with his back, crablike, but a man unmistakably with his own motives for acting like something else. He might have had eyes in the back of his head too, he covered so many directions at once with his swiveling gaze.

That's what surprised me. Having cleared his view of any inhibiting sight with one wipe of the glass (how he missed me in my naked perch must be a birdwatcher's secret), he didn't look up again until it was all over, as though he assumed that everything going on around him would be naturally swept into the orbit of his own whirling activity, becoming part of the atmosphere of his concentration, a world unto himself. From my distant planet, I possessed the more elucidating perspective that made of his fumbling with the proverbial problem—the narrow opening of the gate, the massive, ungainly body of the steer—something pathetic and monstrous, like looking through both ends of a set of opera glasses at once.

So, if his graceful dispatching of the bulky steer through the needle's-eye opening in the fence gave me cause for grudging admiration, the abrupt spectacle of the steer crashing back through the fence confirmed my belief in the folly of all such acts. No man can control the outcome of his deeds, however small or inconsequential. So that's why I feel entitled to my contemptuous opinion. The act of releasing one steer, in addition to its flagrant illegality, is worse yet because it succumbs too shamelessly to the temptation to transform the world merely by manipulating the scale of things: a temptation that for the most worldly-wise of us is simply the palest puff of smoke from the genie's dented lamp and unworthy of notice. But then I was overwhelmed by the subtle symmetry of my thoughts: from the smallest portal of the body the spore of disease is released to pollinate a vast flowering life proffered all around it. Was that what I was witnessing here? I asked myself.

Even from my dizzying height, with the wind pumping water from my teary eyes, flooding the surface until it became a thick distorting lens of crocodile grief, even with the sun smiling on my tears and shivering my sights into a confusing panoply of glassy shards, I saw that it was Moertle down below.

MONOLOGUE OF THE SPOTTED DOG

We scramble away from the scene of the crime. My master is hobbling over the hoof-printed ruts as we re-

trace the fatal steps of the herd through sinuous alley-
ways. His gait isn't helped by the converging horns of his
dilemma where they remain stuffed into the front pockets
of his trousers; and as though they are the enormous
thumb and forefinger of a disciplinary hand, he is pulled
angrily along by his own trouser front. Though the pain-
fulness of this forced march is evident in the whiteness
that falls over his face like a starched handkerchief and the
wetness soaking it through, at the corners of his mouth a
smile is beginning to gather the lips like the tassled purse
string cinched in the moment of the gambit rewarded.

Bark, bark. But no one hears.

Left short-handed, the sheriff contemplated the dimen-
sions of his problem alone from the silent cab of the
truck. He could only surmise that such a steer must have
been plucked from its corral between two unearthly fingers, rotated high above the stockyards by an arm flexing
through broken clouds, and dropped on a carefully
marked line of sight, to have landed like this—head first
in the perfect circle of the well. Perfect bullseye? Accident
of nature?

The sheriff preferred to believe that the vision of the
spotted haunch canted above the stone wall of the well
was tendered from the incensed chambers of some pure,
priestly divination rather than from the democratic arena
of pure chance where everything must be accepted without dissent. Lured by the spectacle of so many awestruck
children gathered silently around the perimeter of the
abandoned well, the sheriff himself was tempted to take
refuge in the aura of mystery, to fish from this enigma

with long leisurely tugs of consciousness until all impatience for an answer flowed out of himself and into the snapping jaws of whatever hovering life stood at the other end of his thoughts.

But he had his job to do. The line with which he finally fished the carcass out of the well was braided as thickly as the intestinal cord knotted at his own cramped waist and attached to a grumbling winch in the bed of the truck. The tips of the long horns, when they snapped off against the wall of the shaft, made no sound at the bottom of the well. The body of the truck lifted buoyantly against the freed weight of the dead animal. Hoisted by its hooves, the carcass in the sunlight appeared indistinguishable from the livid side of beef basking in a glint of the butcher's fine cutlery.

Shielding his eyes from the lowering stroke of the sun, deliberating in the shadow of the pendant carcass, surveying the press of children around the flanks of the truck, the sheriff finally passed judgment. "You who have patted the flying haunch of the carcass for your good luck must report to Dr. Hugo Face for examination. Walk with your hands clasped behind your backs until you reach the full troughs of washing water. Take care you don't let the movements of your fingers get tangled up with the movements of your lips until you are shed of the contagious skin and you are not telling anything with your touch. I know the law."

As the truck's engine breathed awkward life into the swinging carcass, the wheels spat dust into the shocked, open eyes and veiled the blunted horns, the sheriff passed the legion of small children marching single file as he had arranged them. Passing at the head of the line, the sheriff

shot one finger out of the cab window striking the target
he had set for them with a resonant command.

There, at the other end of the abandoned street, the
doctor's eye moved like a bug over water across the circular eyepiece of his microscope.

The boardinghouse steps were swept of the sounds of
children when Moertle returned. Finding the familiar
loose boards that accompanied the notes of his song, he
was forced to step up and down again and to repeat the
last verse before he realized that today no shrill antiphony
would ring from the landing above, "Lillifalura Fallura
lures me. . . ." The staircase leading up three stories in six
sections supported only his own weight of silence.

A single blond thread of sunlight spiraled down from
the crown of the house, the visible relic of a children's
story long since precipitated out of the air of its telling.
Moertle's next step onto the shiny flatbed of a toy truck
removed him from the contemplation of present things as
abruptly as the slip of the mind that brings the story back
from memory. But when he recovered his balance, lifting
himself from his back at the level of a child's eye, he was
crowded by a world of objects that might have leapt out
of the shifting distance of the fall itself. A doll's head was
tied to a stick and the stick planted between two warped
floorboards. The floorboards themselves were slick with
the perspiration of a handful of scattered marbles. A flat-
headed soldier, crossed with shiny black enamel straps
and with a cherubic face the size of a bloody fingerprint,
contemplated the ceiling from the inside of a shoe. The

blue truck was turned upside-down against the wainscoting, its wheels spinning soundlessly.

All around him, Moertle surveyed the empty shells of so many childish preoccupations, hollowed out as the skin of his own hearing. It now had become the heavy fossil of a silence that could last forever.

Only a noise like the faint dropping of spadefuls of damp earth excavated the reluctant contours of his disappointment. Outside, the street was abandoned to the massive footfall of the afternoon sun pacing from one end to the other in infinitely slow and therefore virtually silent steps. Inside, a sound persisted like footsteps so small they would never reach their destination. He had already passed two floors and reflected with the anxious daring of a man holding a revolver to his temple, that they were empty chambers. So he cocked his ears toward the uppermost floor of the boardinghouse. If it had not been completely abandoned, perhaps it harbored only the illusory human presence of a shade flapping against a broken window. A hand to the ear merely confused the identity of the sound, necessitating another footstep, a stiffening of the upper body until it carried the febrile tension of the tapping insect antennae, a held breath.

Another shovelful of damp earth. Then an expulsion of breath like the sound of the victim exhaling laboriously from the bottom of the grave.

Moertle was already halfway up the last flight of stairs. As the sound grew between his ears, he began to enjoy the imminence of the pulsing vision that would burst upon him at the moment his head, his eyes, cleared the final landing of the staircase.

Even with the expectation that, like the victim struggling at the bottom of the grave, he might be met only by the boot heel of his tormentor, he lifted himself over the final obstacle.

Naked, on all fours, tail in the air, blood in her face, was Lilli. And as Moertle's head lifted into view, she collapsed onto the floor from which he at once realized she had raised herself in the first place only to throw herself back, belly first, a fish of insufficient size for whatever appetite stormed within her. She did not see Moertle's face where he fumbled with it in the shadows like a ball of blown glass too delicate to bear handling. The chastising sound of her stomach against the resistant floorboards made Moertle feel the presence of his own fingertips against his skull as an irresistible will of destruction. Because, red as it was, he saw how Lilli's stomach swelled with a force that was inner and no doubt craning its brittle neck against the harsh blows of the floor.

Moertle knew the signs of childbearing from its earliest growth and could not bear the phantasmagoria of the broken egg evoked in the violence of vellum against wood, the belly whitening inside a wreath of blood like a protruding skull.

So, letting his own face fall through the brittle light of the attic room, feeling for the fragile round of the egg instead, Moertle caught Lilli in his arms.

But the sound of a fumbled bauble crashing against the floor could not be avoided as man and woman rolled together against a flaking wall; Moertle's hands across Lilli's flexing stomach pulled as tightly as though he were fitting a hat over his own head. Drenched in the sweat of her exertions, Lilli was smaller than she had ever seemed

in his arms, somehow reborn out of the gesture by which
he reached out to her and now a burden on his hands
that would grow inexorably heavier, like the man who
leaps from a high window embracing a clock weight.

For her part, she was pacified. Lilli's eyes were illuminated by the new dawn she coaxed with her unexpected
question: "Then you want this child to come?"

Moertle was already weeping, already shielding his eyes
against the pink shell cracked from within, the life protruding into the air of his own breathing, syphoning it
off from his own lungs, swelling in his direction with
fingers that can already pick at the surface of the shallow
face like the most private hand in a mirror.

My Papa tells us to press our fingers against our lips
because our mother is sleeping. But these are the fingers
we took from the hide of the dead steer. The doctor says
that the hide of the steer is like a thick and curling tongue
that can suck us into its heaving cavity. So I have told
them to hold their fingers away from their lips as though
they were the birthday candles to be blown out.

All of us know that my Papa is sitting by the bed until
she can lift her head from the pillow. Then he will follow
his own footsteps home. There will be nothing left since
the dog follows behind, sniffing up the traces of my
Papa's presence. A wet, black strawberry, the dog's nose
bristles with nerve endings that must travel all the way
back to the soft eyes, smoothing and straightening themselves through the dilated pupils and passing even further
back to where my Papa sits gathering the threads into his
weaving hands.

104

From the outside of his house, I have seen him just so, sitting in the windowglass that is as big as my two hands. This is what he says: "I am the one who gathers the threads in the tapestry. Mine are the tightest knots that artistry can bear. My knots are holding the pattern like the knuckles of a clenched fist. Not a single thread will escape into its own loosening design wagging the sassy tail of a disobedient dog."

But this time when he leaves I will tie myself to his footsteps so closely that I could be the dog's tail. This time he will not escape the cage of my ten fingers. Though I have followed him before, I have always lost him. His steps were too quick for me. His arm was too long and held me off. And when he finally reached for me in my dark disguise, his hand was so unfamiliar. In future, I will have more to tell.

But as preparation for my own, I must remember how my Papa began his story.

"You are too many," he said, stroking with both arms to keep himself afloat among so many crowding children, "but I know how to wrap you into one. And if I don't I know where to find the door," his eyes reaching out to my Mama, seizing her face with the swiftness of any thieving hand.

The square black suitcase stood at his feet where the dog should have been. It was fastened with silver-tongued clasps. It bulged black as a bruise. Only in expectation that the sides of the suitcase would burst from the heavy breath trapped within (hot as a lizard in its burrow) did we vow to be still. Some of us even pricked our ears to the faint scratching that we knew must be coming from within the suitcase if our Papa's promise was good: Who could wait for it to be opened?

But when we were confronted with the sides split, the backbone of the squat suitcase cracked and splayed, the silver tongues clucked once and for all, we recognized only what was most familiar. A boy our size, hair in his eyes, freshly pinched cheeks, lips, knuckles, knees, outfitted like a range rider but all of him wooden. And especially where the jaw seemed to bite into the base of his neck or where the limbs hung loosely as lengths of freshly tied sausage, the blade of the axe lay invisibly on the bright hue of his skin.

Because we now knew that nothing alive could come from a suitcase, the murmur that my Papa had quelled with open hands began to curve its back against this disappointment, churning up the surface of our tranquillity.

We were twelve children more tentacled than an octopus and yet as compact and singular as the loneliest monster of a deserted sea bottom.

On my Papa's knee, the wooden doll was even more lifeless than he had appeared lying flat with arms folded over his chest, framed by the crepe ruffle at the bottom of the suitcase.

My Papa's eyes were already startled by the commotion beginning to rise in us on massive haunches, stretching, loosening its jaw in a hungry yawn. Birds in the trees are not so skittish as the black pupils in my Papa's eyes, pecked as they are by the jittery movements of children all around him. So he tried to work more quickly. He straightened the angle of the doll on his knee. One hand disappeared inside the back of the wooden doll. He pushed his knee further forward between the boy's dan-

gled legs. But by the time he had settled the weight on
his knee, he was struggling against Prissy and Moira
hanging on his trouser legs, reaching for his free hand
where it was attempting to clear the wooden throat. Behind him, his chair back creaked with the weight of
someone climbing. Another snatched his shoulder. And
though he surely itched to sweep them away with one
wave of his hand, and though he surely looked like a man
mindful only of the hand that is unavailable to swat the
dizzying fly from his face, he occupied that hand with
rubbing the wooden doll's torso, faster and faster like a
boy himself, wishing on an old Arabian lamp. But the
boy was no longer seated passively above my Papa's protruding knee. Because the knee was jumping angrily and,
in collaboration with the rubbing hand, was clearly
arousing the wooden body to my Papa's defense. My
Papa might have cried out: "Boy, see how I am mo-
lested? Show loyalty to your father or stay no longer at
my side."

Instead the boy spoke. The rapid clack of the wooden
jaw might have eaten the fingers that clutched my Papa's
distraction then, they were so quickly withdrawn into
amazed contemplation of this miracle of speech.

Prissy and Moira at his knees and Fanny on his back
slid into a heap on the floor, their attention seized by
recognition of what they heard. Papa's own hand came
loose from its entanglement with Darla's knotting fingertips as these children fell to clutching after their own ears
to hear the miraculous voice, if it should be offered again.
And we pushed together in front, all of us to see if the
wooden eyes would burn with the passion of the strenuous voice. For the voice filled the boy's face as hugely as

the axehead where it bites the wedge-shaped mouth that feeds it. The eyelashes shuddered once, to fan the flame and were lit with a word.

"Fire. Fire has a tongue to tell my story with tonight." The clacking jaw receded behind the soft swelling voice, like the bone under a bruise becoming less real to the touch. And his story left us glowing because it was about a house that burned.

A boy turned from the reflection of himself in a black pool. His eyes were still wet with the concentration that had held him to a watery surface when, turning toward the house, the distance of wavy heat that undulated between himself and the far-flung door created the illusion of a wading foot shattering the calm depth of his contemplation. Then the shivering light blew black at him like smoke off a birthday cake. Behind the smoke, where his eye could penetrate, he saw the flame, red and looking back at him through tears in the smoky curtain. The fire behind the smoke was the roaring monster of his dreams, brewed in darkness as he always suspected, always lurking where he could not see. Working its tongue in the labors of a vast ingestion, the fire grew in inverse proportion to the shrinking pile of blackening white clapboards, pulverized bricks and falling beams. For by the time the boy could push himself through what seemed an infinitely folded curtain of smoke, everything he could remember about his home was blackened by the magician's cape. Where the edge of it lifted above his brow for a moment, he realized the transformation beneath was so total that he would never be able to unravel a single thread of its magic. His head was baked in an oven of shame. His legs staggered under a weight of intense heat. So many flames leapt from falling windows he could not tell which ones contained the dancing figurines of his mama and papa breathing as though behind glass, alive as the breath of the glassblower struggling toward immobility.

Awed by the fragility of the life falling all around him, the boy could only pit himself against the now towering flames. Only he preserved a vivid enough image of what stood behind the flames so that something would be left if they were blown out. Alone in its presence he believed himself a perfect match for fire. He swelled his cheeks to bursting, pulled the lids over his bubbling eyes, sucked stomach, liver and bowels into the hot grip of his lungs, stoppered his ears with two fingers and suddenly, deliberately deflated himself in a single stiff torrent of air that was not as forceful as a fist in a pillow. Then empty, coughing up the last percussive bullets of air and at last compelled to inhale, he felt the indrawn breath as hotly as a flaming bird darting to cover in his mouth, fanning the flames with the ever more convulsive blows of its wings in the breathy darkness. He closed his mouth in time to snag a brittle bird's foot with his lip like a bent pin heated in the halo of a matchhead. The boy ached and sweated. Now he heard the wings of the bird flapping louder and more violently against the sides of the house, beating them down. The boy sweated and burned. Inside and outside were fused by the melting light of the sun. The boy burned and finally cried. When he cried, the tears were only a panting breath on his cheeks, he was still so close to the flame.

But being so wrung out by the fleet hands of catastrophe he could not fly away. He did not turn his face away but urged from the sweating tears the calm that follows every physical exertion, until all preoccupation with the heat of his body evaporated like mist on the glass of his eye, leaving him calm and protected from the fire's most violent explosions by the cool distance of his gaze.

He was unflinching and he took it all in on nimble fingertips of attention, fitting each falling detail into a pattern of his memory where the house was still whole and presented the template for future contemplation. So, as the last supporting boards of the frame house were collapsing, the boy was building with meticulous tweezered movements of his mind, making a hot glue on his tongue, using the leverage of his lowering eyelids to think, to lift into place each remembered particle of its wooden construction as he had once seen an old man at a table reassembling a sailing ship emptied from a bottle. When the flame fell to scavenging the last unpicked bones of the house, the steep angles and vaulted space of the boy's longing rose up before him as high as the reach of the flame. His concentration stiffened his neck as though he were balancing a jug of precious liquids on the crown of his head. And the shadow that fell from these labors caught him first by his ankles, a flash flood of feeling that he would remain immersed in for the rest of his life, like a species forced to return to the waters of its primitive evolution.

When the hilltop where the house had been could be seen like a volcanic eruption from the sunken streets of the town, the men with their water wagons and the women with their tearful eyes arrived too late to dampen the flame in the boy's face.

They found him staring on the blackened threshold of catastrophe, but at an angle above the wreckage that only the smoke still clung to for its support, admitting no window on the sky above. Women gave him their breasts like the drooping heads of sunflowers to water with his tears, and small children were encouraged to take his hand, to lead him away to some more consoling sight or humor of childish intimacy. But the boy held firm, his concentration driven through him like a stake into the ground. Finally the men had to come with sooty hands and blankets thick enough to protect their bare arms from the boy's teeth.

I saw then that the wooden jaws of the doll bore no teeth, and that the boy in the story was none other than my Papa himself, though no part of him was wooden or grained with the secret identity of the tree.

So you see I can tell a story, too. Never again will my Papa's footsteps be too quick for my tongue to tell. I follow one word with another and because they come from my mouth I will know the taste of him like his dog knows the smell of him. When next he walks away from our home I will already be there where his back is turned, forming the words in my mouth as he tells himself which direction to take out of our sight.

While my Mama lies still in her bed, my Papa might well be carved out of the wood of the chair he sits on. But underneath the stiff expression he wears on his face, the muscles are tugging on the bones to go.

"How is a child born after it has already been beaten?"

Hustus Moertle confides the question to me without a hint of the fear that I know is plunged into him like a virulent innoculation. Because his question does not so-

111

licit a prognosis. Rather it makes one, about himself: that he is intolerant of the conception of the child
but fearful to interfere in the division of cells. That the
woman's irrational act—beating the fetal blood against
the floor—is like a pinched nerve holding him in check
against any further movement but enacting an infinite
repetition of the motion that set it on, so that he will
now suffer from it forever himself.

I have examined the patient as well. I have seen how
Lilli's breath is moving inside her, licking the child's
wounds, swaddling it with warm fur, restoring the anatomy of motherhood to its proper function. And I can see
that my doctoring will be urgently required—but not for
the child who will be born alive—for the mother who is
carrying more than she shows with the exertions of her
belly. Moertle does not see this. Moertle has cause to
worry but it has nothing to do with the leaping life of the
newborn that he says already causes an irremediable pain
of memory. And he squeezes his lemony eyes to say it, as
though proof of his statement will be manifest in the two
acidic droplets that are meant to sour my good humor.

But I am not at all a captive of the illusory symptoms
conjured with unsubtle motions of the flesh. I attend
more closely to the words themselves than to the laborious gesture Moertle makes of pouring them out of an
ungainly clay pot. By listening to the words that tell of it,
I will recognize any ailment in its most lurid disguises.
Though Moertle's words evoke overbright pictures of the
woman stitched up in her tight skin of milk, breaking her
taut stomach against the floor, bursting with light, such
pictures slowly gather the shadows of his own guilt, the
dusty patina of his own activity in the corral, and the

112

memory of his own crime. Because sometimes one thing means another. So when Moertle confides his paralysis at the thought of the bulging new life, I think I understand: I do not ask him about his job. I whisper nothing of what I have seen with my own eyes from the shivering tower of the windmill. I need not remind him that one of the deputies is already dead, that the other is wrestling with a sweaty angel, that the points of contact in this struggle are marked by white blisters boiling up a salty sea. We both know the next tide might carry him away. All these things are already spoken for when Moertle reiterates his distaste for children, his especial fear of a child born of severe chastisement, and his belief that every child is already born with a fist clenched against the breaking of the water.

Because sometimes one thing means another and the only way to know it is to believe it, as nothing else makes sense. To know one world is always to know another sunk beneath it, like fish through drinkable water. In just this way do I know that hoof and mouth is a disease of four-legged creatures; but the distance from foot to mouth is a short one and may be devoured by any mouth articulate enough to explain how the mind can be affected by the body—even the body that is not one's own. The foot holds no advantage over the mouth (even on the open plain) when the mouth is in motion. The mouth covers greater distances. It runs faster even than the earth turning underfoot.

Withdrawing my disinfected hand from the extended body of this sleeping woman, I am reluctant to say that it is a disease of the mind she carries upon her heavy eyelids. But in time she will tell me herself and, when I have confirmed her symptoms, I will not be inhibited from tracing the steps of her contagion to the sediment of hard-shelled hoofprints built up like a shelf of barnacles in the baked mud of the corral. Hoof and mouth is a disease of four-legged creatures but as long as upright men sometimes crawl, they are stooping low enough to communicate with the scent of the trail. Perhaps the child cowering under the delicate earpiece of Lilli's navel will be born of such furtive communication.

My Moertle waits for the train to appear on the horizon as though he were contemplating a gopher hole. His eye is quick and stealthy and as small against the horizon as the gopher looking out. Yet the abrupt appearance of the train always catches him by surprise, gobbling up the pea-sized pupil more quickly than it can dilate to encompass a shattering scene.

The station depot is little more than a backyard of the slaughterhouse where my Moertle paces out the arrival of the herd with his own two feet, measuring the length of a single steer over and over. Each boxcar, kicked with the force of eighty hooves, rattles over the track with a tenuous grip on the blazing rails. Many times my Moertle has noted that the engineer's face peers from the windows of the ancient locomotive with the faraway look of one who has been swallowed by a thrashing whale. When the train finally heaves itself against the sides of the loading dock, the engineer exposes the white length of his throat beneath the amber light of a tilted bottle.

When the air of the station begins to heat with the stench of animal waste, the boxcars burst open. It is, my

Moertle explains, as though the expanding breath of excrement were the first shock wave of the explosion to come. One by one the cars are drawn before an upthrust wooden ramp. The ramp is fed directly into the outermost corral of the convoluted network of corrals through which the slow regurgitation of animal parts commences. The boxcar lifts on creaky springs as though a single body were shifted off balance, because the three hundred cattle move as one from the confinement of clapboard construction to the confinement of whitewashed lattice fencework.

My Moertle notes that their passage from one wooden confinement to the other is oblivious of the towering forest that rears up in the most meticulous human scrutiny of both. The stillest pool in the forest reflects the truest scene.

My Moertle stands still against a swirling current of cattle disembarking from fifteen cars. The electric prod sets up an unusual rhythm in the palm of his hand. Tuneless, a tension that will not be discharged, it travels to his head and lodges behind his eyes. The sun strikes there too, heavy as the bottom of a hot skillet. But my Moertle performs his duty without wincing, without complaint.

So, in the late afternoon of every Wednesday, my Moertle reports to his assigned place in the deepest reservoirs of sunlight and stagnant air that have collected beside the railroad track. He is his own puppeteer. The fingers of one hand are threaded with complicated hand signals that he must.convey to the engineer in order to avert disaster. Memory holds the strings like a wet fist behind the throbbing light of his headache. He never misses his mark, and the train has never slipped off his gesturing fingertips into a heap of twisted wreckage.

Yet today my Moertle's sober punctuality goes unrewarded. Only a dry wind rushes past the platform.

Several other hands are kneeling around a pair of clicking dice in the shade of a cattle ramp. To my Moertle, the sound of the toss is like a man getting ready to spit. The cry that goes up after every click of the dice raises a little dustcloud.

The same dust is twitching spider legs inside my Moertle's nose. The windshield of a parked truck is already caught in its web and entangled with the yellow forklift waiting on its flank. The web stretches over this lingering afternoon, spins itself out in fine gold filaments and finally hangs limply in the dying air. Only my Moertle's vigilant breathing sways the tapestry of unmoving men and things.

A whistle off the horizon calls everyone to the edge of the platform to stare down the darkling chute of the railroad track. My Moertle is already there, scratching the isinglass dusk to see better how the silver locomotive will catch fire as it rounds the last mile of sunlit track. But it is already so dark that the eyes have to lean on the ears to see.

Or else something is blocking their view of the track, casting the last slithering shadow of the afternoon that is actually its own bodily self drained of all light. And before a still distant sound of firecrackers is muffled, as though by the palm of the hand that must have held them too long, my Moertle thinks he can see the briefest silhouette of horn and humped back, touched off like a spark to a fuse by the gleam of roaring steel behind it.

No other sound travels the length of track to where the throng of hands are stampeding their ears over the dark precipice of the loading dock. For several minutes, they stand silently with their senses cocked in the direction of the invisible horizon. Then their concentration recoils back upon them with questions about what they have just heard and with plans of action, guesses about the outcome of this sudden night. Some vote to head out immediately, sifting the darkness with the long shafts of their automobile headlights for whatever might be buried under the blanketing silence. Others who boasted more experience with the illusory distances of night recounted the ruses to which one falls prey at sunset: the footsteps that sound behind but leap out in front, the cry for help that fades as one steps closer, until the ground yawns underfoot, swallowing consciousness whole.

"The darkness is a pulled curtain," one spoke from under a steep hat brim. "Whatever you take from behind the curtain you are stealing from that other hand."

My Moertle listened negligently to the talk that went on all night. My Moertle stood, patiently alert for the first finger of sunlight that would point out what had happened, though he knew that no one examining the heaps of wreckage illuminated on both sides of the track would understand the cause of the catastrophe. For only by examining the cattle brand stamped on its haunch would anyone guess that the steer crumpled under the front wheels of the upset locomotive was not part of the herd that had spilled out at the moment of impact and now ranged out around the wreck without any hope of being corralled. Only the man patient enough to examine every detail would finally come upon a clue—a double bar crossed by a shepherd's crook—to tell a tale by. The rest of the herd that would become invisible as it soaked through the porous flatland of the horizon would have exhibited a black "M" lassoed by a broken circle on their running flanks. My Moertle tells himself what must have happened:

Hours behind schedule, despairing of the light, the engineer must have pushed the throttle to its limit. His cargo swayed behind him, each wild swing of the long tail balancing against its opposite, the entire train held to the winding track by the delicate symmetry of its unstable movements. The sound of the ties shifting beneath the wheels of the train warned of a dangerous undercurrent disturbing the waters of this swimmer's night.

And when the engineer's red eye was burning a hole in the horizon, leaping to his destination like a spark to a nest of dry shavings, he failed to notice what was right under his nose. Though its shape was indistinguishable from the cargo stampeding behind the trainman's back, the steer crossing the track ahead of him presented an unavoidable obstacle to all forward motion. As it struck the brown flank, the nose of the locomotive seemed suddenly to lose the strong scent that impelled it in its forward motion. It lifted abruptly as though it were about to sink into deep water, turning all balanced horizontal motion into vertical inertia so that the entire length of the train behind it was folded upon itself in an accordion press of steel and smoke. One discordant collision of notes from the smashed accordion and there was silence, steam, a sound of dripping and at last a bellowing from the animal lungs that spread out from the scene of disaster like a pool of blood.

118

By the time the truckloads of ready hands from the slaughterhouse yard arrived to grasp the full dimension of this disaster, only a few thirsty head of cattle were still drowned in the violent shadows of the wreckage. The baked terrain revealed no imprint of the rest of the herd. The engineer sitting in full sun, riding the back of the jackknifed caboose, was shaking an empty bottle over his head, predicting that rain would wash the sight of it all away.

My Moertle, driver of the first of the battered pickups, reflected that it hadn't rained as long as his dog had been licking his cheek. Since nothing big enough to haul it away ever drove in this direction, my Moertle knew the wreckage would remain, rustproof, flaking a bit under the picking fingers of the sun, perhaps becoming a reservoir for dust, but it would remain intact and as large on the horizon as though it had been there forever. The thought smiled in the corners of his mouth. It crouched there while he made sure that he had missed no clue that could tell them which way the herd was traveling from here.

"A helicopter's the thing for this job," one of the men volunteered from the bed of the truck where he had slept through the night to be ready for the first foray. But my Moertle's foot on the brake stamped the words out in a cloud of dust that left them coughing behind the cab. For this reason, he didn't hear the rejoinder that would have stretched the grin even wider across his face, as the men unloaded themselves from the truck: "They'll turn up in town. There's no other water for 150 miles. A cow's nose is tuned to it like the radio. We'll have them walking into our living rooms, as many as we need for an old-fashioned rodeo again."

As some of the hands bent to the futile task of shifting wreckage with their own muscle, my Moertle took the scene in with the satisfaction of a man who has just eaten well. The wetness on his lip was stronger than the sun and seemed to seal him off from the contrary will of the elements.

The doctor alone was witness to this spectacle of private contentment. Carried out aboard the last of the pickup trucks and at the last moment, having heard of the probability of disaster from a shrill crier in the street, having run with belly in hand, having caught a quick hand from the open back of the departing truck, he was not surprised that his hunch had paid off.

Watching my Moertle's back, which did not bend to the labors all around him, did not honor the professional obligation to calculate the losses he surveyed, Dr. Face raised his eyebrow and fell into the attitude of prognosis.

"Only one man stands to benefit from such confusion."

Thinking of the coincidence of cattle falling from a train, cattle falling into the streets, the doctor heard himself writing it all down in the scratchy pages of his personal diary—confident of the day he should be asked to transcribe it all into the public record, blackening the strictly ruled columns of the indictment, whitening the eye of the beholder.

MONOLOGUE OF THE SPOTTED DOG

I am running behind the shotgun report of the truck's exhaust pipe, stretched to full stride, mouth open, tail up, skewered and sizzling on the trail of white smoke: the scent is warming like a bed of coals under my nose. Though the truck hurtles forward, my master is staring back at me to see have I caught it yet—the first odor of livestock fuming over a horizon, that shimmers with the glare of the rising sun like a freshly scrubbed serving plate.

All the other eyes in the truck are pitched forward against the brightening windshield, but my master stares persistently backward at the white foam, the curdled bark, rising on the vibrant strings of my throat and the white thumbs pressing against the pupils of my eyes until they have popped. The pads of my feet touch the ground without feeling, though I am carrying the extra weight of pebbles that catch between the toes when they land. And the wetness of my nose travels back to my mouth, baiting my thirst. My rib cage is a bellows for the warming day.

Still my master gives the one behind the wheel no signal to stop, but with his own eyes urges me forward. He wants me to experience the distance as a scent that evaporates faster under the panting scrutiny of one approaching on faster and faster feet.

The rain came as a wonder to all, furrowing brows, making eyes blink. The tilt it imposed on disbelieving faces left them off balance in the most familiar routines of everyday living. Scrutiny of the sky relieved the obsession with the cracking earth that had swallowed many useful objects small enough to go unnoticed. Though it wasn't a steady downpour, the rain came daily, as tears to the successive layers of peeling onion.

Rivulets began to form and people began to leave footprints behind them, the inscription of every human act there for anyone to read. Every trembling declivity of earth nervously cupped its watery treasure as though to disguise its greediness with the gesture of giving it up. The overflowing pools began the subtle rearrangement of things that flow downstream. One place would be carried to another in chips and flecks of paint, shreds of paper, dustballs, puffs of fur, all accumulating where they were never expected. In the stock corrals, the earth began to churn and thicken into muddy curds, the man's foot at last clearly distinguishable from the hoof of the four-legged creature.

And in those places where the sodden earth was undisturbed, spiky shoots went up. The surface bristled like an itchy skin blooming with rash. Everyone guessed at the upheaval they couldn't see when the white tips broke the earth's crust and they stood clear of it.

Those who had lived in this district during the time of farming and grazing were old enough to feel the rainwater in their bones, as though under the pumping force of their own heart muscle, the downpour was overflowing into anatomical regions unfit for draining off the lakes of pressure. The old ones sat up in porch chairs with a constant view of the weather, did not sleep, and had an appetite only for dry grains that might absorb some of the seeping moisture. Children who had never seen it before stood out in the rain, soaked it up. They went barefoot where the earth had lost its teeth and sucked the water through their toes onto soft gums. The children did not play in the rain. All waited to know how long it would last.

Moertle waited too, sipping cautiously from a deepening pool of thought. He suspended the schedule of his weekly visits home out of the knowledge that a desert doesn't regenerate overnight. In the foundation hole of the ruined house the shards of a broken mirror would already be sparkling up from the bottom. But the impatient face peering down would only find itself shattered along the uneven surface of the floor. So Moertle would wait patiently until the mirror was made whole again, and hope to find himself all smiles in the blooming landscape that it would reflect around him. A man dry for so long must be wary of mirages as he lowers his face to drink.

The first wave of unusual weather lasted a week. The sky lightened as suddenly as a bird is startled from the treetops—but it would come back to roost, huge, black-winged, sullenly clinging to its perch.

My Papa doesn't see because he doesn't think to. But I am here, as concentrated a presence as his thought that he is alone in this quickstep behind the parading length of the herd. On the opposite side of the fence I have taken my Mama's phrase "thin as a rail" to heart, fitting myself to the narrow shadows of the posts. As I follow the length of the corral, my Papa flickers between the posts as if cast in the light of a guttering flame.

But he doesn't break stride. He might as well be one of them—all headed for the barn door—until he puts his hand out to the tail in front of him, apparently well met. He pulls. He leaps, he changes places with the startled animal. When he is face to face with it, he has the look of a bold defender because he has blocked its path, he is brandishing the electric wand. With it he has cut one off from the rest of the herd. But just as the wand is lowered to the level of its transforming powers, I see that it is my Papa who is cut off from things. The arm that brandishes the enchanted wand falls limp at his side. Though he has not been struck—unless from some recess of the invisible world that endows the power of the wand—it falls out of my Papa's hand, releasing the steer from its nets of frustration. My Papa must turn quickly on his heels to keep up with a gait that wants only to merge with its rhythmic likeness. I must move twice as quickly.

I have never passed through the roaring barn doors before. The noise from within hovers high up in the structure. Anyone who passes through on ground level would be helpless prey to the black bird which must be roosted above. But I do not hesitate to follow my Papa into the din. Last in line, I am thinking only of what will follow.

Out of the loud darkness, softer lights become audible in the numerous activities they illuminate. First a single row of incandescent bulbs threaded along a low ceiling keeps the herd in tow, as though they are being added to an ever more uncountable string of beads. My Papa is no longer following behind but adjacent to and separated from the herd by a low wall. His eye rides along the top of the wall until the corridor it makes with a higher wall—standing five feet off and raised up to the full height of the building—comes to a stubborn halt. At its dead end, the corridor is crowned by a metal bridge. The bridge makes it possible for a man swollen as any bruised body and apparently swathed in bloody bandages, to stand directly above the approaching animal and to pull the fierce head of his hammer over one greased shoulder, the slick head of the hammer kissing the head of each steer violent and true. Though they collapse out of sight beneath the low wall, the cattle do not pile up under the arch of the metal bridge. Neither does the white-coated executioner—who grows larger with each pumping blow—ever reach down one of his inflatable arms to clear a space for his next victim. Then who moves the carcasses?

The answer is not what I expect. It is as I have seen only in the painted pictures of our Father's heavenly way. And it is not for these eyes: not before, but behind the white-coated executioner, the bloody souls of the dead animals ascend, headless, tails sweeping a floor of darkness, rising into a halo of light that fits each like an incongruous hat. How is it that my papa's face greets them from above while I remain below where I have been watching him?

I find the spiral staircase like a bell pull lowered into a well. Each climbing step tolls new recognitions of the noise that fills the upper stories like a hive with honey. Knives, hammers, belts, crash of metal buckets, rattle of chains, spray of water, slosh of boots descend like the swarm kicked loose of its hive. And I am the clumsy wanderer. But keeping my Papa in view above me, ascending the wrought-iron staircase right through the floor of the mezzanine, I can now see that the haltered carcasses have come the same way, except through a different hole. And now I see that my Papa has caught up with them already because he is tethered to something that weighs heavily inside them, something that makes them dance even more lively in their leather halters. The dance step comes so easily to my Papa's restless foot that he might be hanging from his own rope.

And so my Papa is a wriggling worm to the hook that drags the carcasses off their halters, and chugs on its narrow-gauge ceiling track around the perimeter of the mezzanine. I am the gullible fish.

Because where I pursue my Papa's footsteps, I am the one who is harried. I can see that where the fierce steel hook has bitten off the head of the steer it nods in the direction of the reddest violence. The blades of the hide cutters are long and curved and serrated. The tip of the blade inserted under the armpit releases the shoulder as gently as a lady's arm from her fur sleeve, but what is drawn away from the gallantry of the blade is raw. It trembles as any moistened lip beneath the advancing tooth. The bands of cartilage that are exposed like the straps of some supportive undergarment snap, making the body blush down to the wispy tops of the hooves.

Then I think my Papa's mouth has become salty with the unceasing flow of blood, he puckers so. Or a kiss is shedding its skin on his lips, like a moth from its flaming cocoon. Because, though it is advancing on its track, my Papa is pushing his face closer to the side of the carcass, close enough to catch the length of tail when it is snipped, close enough to pocket a white curd of fat, and close enough to the butcher's jovial smile to catch the words from his mouth before I can hear them. My Papa must have taken his nourishment there, since the mouth that releases his own laughter in response opens nearly wide enough to account for the missing head of the steer.

Then I see the resemblance to his Goat, lapping everything in sight. Nose, mouth, tongue buzz in the orbit of the carcass that is usually reserved for the flies. And from this point on, the carcass begins to show the toothmarks of my Papa's lunging shadow more frighteningly with every step he takes to follow.

Even though where I kneel beside a row of metal buckets I am marooned on the last island of sheltering shadow I can still look diagonally across to the adjacent length of mezzanine catwalk and follow my Papa on the bulging whites of my eyes.

When he bows in front of it, the seam that splits across the belly of the carcass heaves a moist sigh. The lips curl away from the wound to disgorge a slick, close, bulbous growth, the cellared fruit of warm dark places. And its warmth sweeps over me in a sweat bubbling up like the effervescence from the uncoiling intestines of the dead animal. My Papa's face, crouching so low beneath the carcass that he might have spewed into the bucket placed there for collecting the sweaty viscera—the stomach, liver, gall bladder, all of the bulging fruit snipped off by the butcher's bright shears—lifts only enough to allow the level in the bucket to rise beneath him. Or maybe his squatting figure invokes the bottom of the bucket as though it would do his bidding. Perhaps that is his purpose in following the cattle through the boisterous doors of the slaughterhouse: that he can dip with this bucket into the dark waters of some secret intent. In a moment his hand will emerge with the key to the mystery, wet and gleaming. Yet over my shoulder I can see the endless row of buckets that I huddle against, brimming with the same soft phosphorous glow that can only be compared with the surface of the eye following its object out of sight. And then my Papa's bucket is dragged away and added to the row beside me as though only to measure out the distance that stretches between us in years and experience as well as shadowy space. I think I will get no closer to my Papa today, that as the carcass swings out of the reach of his long arms so he will lurch ahead of my sights where I cling to the long sleeves of darkness.

But rising from the place where the bucket stands as though he has stood up inside it, my Papa is no longer balanced on his own feet. I can see that something invisible is passing brusquely between himself and the chugging carcass, buffeting his chest, separating him from his purpose, spinning him around with the cow's tail still swinging loosely from one hand as though he were staggering, lost in the heavy blindfold of a children's game.

Assured of the blindfold, I stand up into the light, the better to see what is wrong. But the white-coated attendants at their separate stations of butchery seem to observe nothing unfamiliar. They meet my Papa's eyes and pass him without blinking. Friendly hands perch and fly from his shoulders as though my Papa were communicating with the birds in their trees. And I notice for the first time that the butcher's speech, though feverish and uninterrupted, is inaudible except as the whetting of knife blades, the chugging of the track, the scraping of the buckets along the floor. So if it is going to be so hard to separate one thing from another, I decide that I will be revealed as my unmistakable self.

But when I move close enough to my Papa and am stuck by the revealing light glaring above the cutting tables, he refuses to see me as the helpful child. Nor does he see where he is going, with the cow's tail flickering

128

against the peripheral darkness. And I am sure he does not see.

He falls down. He stands up near the mezzanine railing. He overlooks the empty depth of the building hollow at its center. He turns back toward the train of streaming carcasses. And because I have been holding his trouser leg back from the dizzying rail, when he turns I receive the bat end of his knee, as heavy as any falling body, across the tip of my nose.

At last the long shadow of the executioner's hammer has caught me as well, though it is a white light that flares up through the center of my head.

My Papa is already past me. The silent bat shriek that escapes from my throat calls no one's attention to the spout of thick blood chasing after it. I am inaudible, invisible as the bat itself hanging upside down in the back of my mouth. The blood is over me in a downpour.

But the first cries to fly above the indecipherable din of the butchering are my Papa's, rising where he has stepped past me to hug the last carcass in the long train. At the end of its track, it is being hoisted into the refrigerated atmosphere of the third floor above us. His arms around waxen shoulders are either the fortuitous support for a man who could no longer keep his balance on his own two feet or the deliberate embrace of the dancer with the dance. Through my tears, I see my Papa is crying as the ascending steel hook tears through the collar of gristle and bone that hangs on it, dropping man and beef together to the sawdust floor before any of the white-coated attendants can pull them apart.

More invisible than ever, eclipsed from my view of the scene by the swelling fruit of my own nose and swallowing blood for the first time, I realize that what is inside will one day be outside too. And then my first audible cry soars like the large carrion bird (I had feared it so on the threshold of this building) as it returns to its ominous circling over the fists of the fallen.

When the white bandage raises its hump over the bridge of my nose and I am able to swim off my watery legs onto more solid footing, I return to the pane of my Papa's window glass as big as my two hands and behind which my Papa always reappears glistening and new. Though I cannot press my nose to the glass, I lay one eye like a bobbing roe against the cool transparent undulation where the play of inside and outside becomes an elemental confusion.

Chewing, wagging his head over the shaky tabletop as though he has deliberately denied himself the use of his hands (let alone silverware), my Papa chokes down the last morsel of what was apparently a plate of undercooked meat, though all that remains is a shallow puddle of red juices and the long trembling of the tabletop.

MONOLOGUE OF THE SPOTTED DOG

He throws me a piece of meat already chewed once. It must have grabbed his throat with a fiercer grip than he could hold a fork with if he had held one between his fingers. Remember, he is a skinny man. He doesn't want the food passed forcibly through his narrow passageways. He wants clearance to keep the stops open so that whatever changeable wind blows over him will play an inspirational music to his ears. But I hear him chewing, wet and clacking and without a rhythm that a man could hook his foot to. So I stoop to the savory scrap and sniff out the fermentation of his digestive juices still active as an infestation of maggots. If I take it, they will be on my tongue without knowing the difference.

Lillifalura placed her husband's hands upon the crown of her stomach, where amid the sensations of intelligent life waking to alarm, Moertle could twine his fingers in the downy precocious hairs that had sprouted at the top of her navel. As though the belly had formed prematurely and directly into the newborn's head and the blood were already thinking in the telegraphy transmitted through Moertle's flat palm, he could not bear the contact. But Lilli held his hand to the spot. She told him that the lullaby she sang was for his own uneasy head. It hung from the stalk of his neck, overripe, filling with fluid, though his mouth was dry.

At first he thought that her inability to rise from the sickbed could be laid to the unfamiliar weight of the child gathering like water in a declivity of earth and furrowing it deeper. But he thought that as she exercised herself against that growing weight, as she became accustomed to its shape and hardened to the imprint it made on soft stomach and intestine, that she would finally be able to lift it like the burden of a routine chore to which one naturally bends over time as though it has been taken inside.

"Ingestion is something I know about," said "Dinah the Damsel in Distress", showing him how she had passed the food *through her self, like sand through an hourglass, to replicate the shape of the wasp's stinging metabolism at her own waist.*

She had parted her robe at midlength. Now she fluttered the open wings where they touched her dressing room floor in order to make a low breeze over Moertle's feet.

He had come to see how she was living. For a week she had clapped herself behind the doors of her dressing room without food or drink. Now as she moved closer to him, flapping the wings of the dressing gown ever more strenuously, he saw that she had only this moment risen from the nest of her motives. Behind her the center of the circular bed still held the shape of an enormous white egg where the covers were turned down from the sheets. Moertle understood that it was the imprint of the egg and not the hard of the shell that curved against his eye, making him blink. But above the headboard, the wall plaster was cracked up to the ceiling and he could not be sure that the telltale fragments of shell should not be sought along its edges. And she might have walked through the wall, she eclipsed it so suddenly with the outspread wings of the robe as she closed them over his back.

Lilli lifted her forehead to Moertle's hand. One touch told him it was hotter even than the head that reared up in her stomach. He blew softly upon the perspiring brow, at the same time trying to calm the furnace in his own stomach by feeding it smaller and smaller portions of air. With each breath she took, the images in her dream flickered more vibrantly, the light shining more brightly through them until each was an unquenchable flame.

Up she rose, from a child's hard lap. Her head, she suddenly knew, possessed an autonomous life, somehow free of the burden of arms, legs and torso. The child's face sank beneath her and somehow the upturned gaze conveyed the impression of something struggling for its life beneath the limpid depth of eye water. Finally, Lilli flew high enough above the supplicant's eyes that they flattened into bright reflecting surfaces and she could at last enjoy the sensations of a taller and thinner physical frame than had ever supported such consciousness before—an increase of proportion and a reduction of substance. And when she moved to embrace her Moertle at this distance above the ground, she was dancing, though her dancing feet pushed off from no floor beneath them. The dance was executed as the measured steps of a journey, but she knew she was going nowhere.

When her swimming fingertips reached his shoulders, "Dinah the Damsel in Distress" tried to lean on her Moertle and found him unreceptive. The robe was now at her feet like a discarded leash, freeing the skin to its wildest boundings. She had become more than the woman on the stage. She had become the woman who pushes past the patient, observing eye to embrace the body that shakes. Where her two long legs were stuck into the most squirming portion of her flesh, she gouged her Moertle's sight. She pushed him backward in the attitude of the wounded. He wheeled toward the door. It was handleless to his blind hand. Backed right up to the thick wall of the dressing room, Moertle experienced the changes that occur in the person who cannot see what is in front of him but cannot deny its presence, leaping from the crumbling ledge of one uncertain sense to another, hoping the next one will bear the burden of his disembodied weight.

She had become more than the woman on the stage and he preferred the woman on the stage. He struggled to regain the familiar distance of the audience in their seats. He longed to be swept up into the air of his balcony box, where the plump-

ness of the cushion beneath him was all the flesh he needed to convince himself that he was there.

Then he was reeling backward from imaginary footlights, tripping over the protruded lip of the stage because she was, for all his life, like the nefarious puppeteer reaching out to grab you from behind the billowy curtain. Dinah's hands were spreading over him, covering him with the darkness that fits like a pithy ball into the cupped palm of the hand.

Lilli clung to her Moertle, the dream hanging on her back like the collapsed weight of a parachute. She was still dancing, but now the dance step resounded against sturdy floorboards. Her eardrums might have been absorbing the impact directly, though her feet were bare and could not have made a sound greater than the slap of the tongue against the roof of the mouth. And yet the percussive rhythm of the dance told her she had alighted on the ground. When she looked down, she could see her Moertle's rattlesnake boot tips cutting wedges of air beside her as silent as aging cheese, and then she could hear the taps of the boot heels when he leaned away from her. There must have been firm ground there when he used his boot heels to exert leverage on her arms, pulling her toward him, making her sweat. And because she had plunged from a breathless height, she felt the weight of the lower atmosphere as a drag on her spinning waist. She began to feel the flush first in her toes and fingers. Heat and weight congealed into a single sensation, thickening the faster her partner twirled her. She wanted to stop but the momentum of the dance blurred the walls of the room until they clenched her in a black fist. She tried to let go of her partner, only to realize that it was his grip on her that held her to the dance.

It was the squeezing hand she felt over her entire body, as though she were cupped in the potter's warm palm, a ball of softening clay ready to be kneaded. The knuckles hurt her, first imprinting the sensations that she associated with the bulging side of the finished pot. The long pulling fingers of heat began to smear the lines of definition in her separate limbs, drawing the perspiration from her joints, greasing the motion toward oblivion. The pulse that squeezed her temples pressed its fingers closer together. Her eyes were brimming and then coursing in muddy channels over the rise of cheekbones. Her nose was a formless curd flung into orbit on the perimeter of the whirling dance. She felt the dome of her skull collapsing within. Her cheeks met inside her mouth like clapping hands. And finally the opposing fingertips that pulsed against her temples touched with the slipperiness of a smeared thumbprint.

And Moertle himself felt his whole body growing slick with the buttery contact of Dinah's skin. Because she covered him, he burned with more combustion over the coals of his embarrassment.

And yet it was only with her hand that she was holding him, untangling the knot between his legs and letting the threads unravel in every direction. Seated on the floor with his backbone as stiff behind him as though it grew inside the wall, he began to understand how he was being devoured. Her head had replaced her hand with a hold as strong. But the heat from her mouth had delivered him, he was sure, into the hot grip of her lunging intestine. Hers was the breath that dissolves and makes a finer mesh of the sweated tissue than can the tooth with all its shredding sharpness. She had pulled him into her deepest pit, where the organs are clustered like fer-

135

menting grapes, where one thing is indistinguishable from the others because all the surfaces are porous with the exchange of heat, and all sensation is quickened to one tissue wall collapsing symmetrically upon another. Pressed so, Moertle could only wait for the oppressive boot heel of consciousness to lift, having put out the flame at least.

Sprawling with the abrupt motion of something squeezed out between tense fingers, Lilli jolted her Moertle out of his dream. His ear still burned with its communication to Lilli's upturned belly, where it had lain through the night. Now, with the earpiece lifted as though from the cradle of its incessant ringing, Lilli was released into the first easeful arms of undreaming sleep.

Now they are coming off the plain to fall at our feet, many more than we have ever counted before. So many they might have been standing in line to enter, one by one, a moving train, without an engineer to lunge on the brake handle, without a track to keep them moving beyond our hazy streets, where we are left blinking our eyes in the perpetual dust clouds kicked up by the heels of catastrophe.

When we open our eyes again, the bovine genii are suddenly in our midst breathing their last or already drained to the last drop—like the one whose eyes pierced themselves with their own reflection when he plunged his head impulsively through the shimmering window glass of an abandoned storefront. That is where I discovered him submerged in the silence of a street where signs are posted to discourage the wayward populace—bored with their own stoop and too easily carried away by the impatient tapping of their own feet.

Did the tongue touch the wetness of the window glass before the hard head of the steer broke the watery illusion into a rainbow of prismatic shards? Did the jaw, which must have dropped open in surprise, cause the whispering lips of the wide throat to open, taunting the animal's thirst with the dripping of its own blood? Would the pooled blood have slaked the animal's thirst? These were questions that I posed for Moertle as he stepped around the carcass, doing the duty of his inspection. He had to pass back and forth through the unhinged door of the storefront because the carcass lay inside and outside both. Where the hole gaped around the interior darkness, the animal had fallen halfway through the glazed surface deeper than his reflection must have seemed in the glass. The front end, facing the back wall of the room might have been kneeling in a prayer for light, except that the long gash running from the back of the throat to the middle of the speckled chest was itself brimming with an effulgent and livid sun that would never set.

Moertle's eyes paced back and forth over the jackknifed backbone of the carcass until his look was furry with the contemplation of such a heavy hide.

"Well, he's not one of ours, is he?," fingering the bright threads of the cleaver stitched onto the pocket flap of his denim jacket. "No sign of a number. No mark of the corral on him. He might have been coming for us but I can't take responsibility for the carcass he left behind. It's a cargo that's never been delivered maybe, but even that speculation is out of my jurisdiction."

"It's a full sack of pestilence," I might have replied, "like the one slung invisibly over your shoulder every day when I watch you stooping behind the herd in the corral.

You don't even know what it is that weighs you down."
But I just tapped him on the shoulder, I just nodded to
the floor, pointed at the shattered crowns of the animal's
hooves. I curled back the lips and traced the outline of a
lump stillborn inside the animal's still swelling tongue. I
pulled one eyelid back far enough to display the yellow
irises like tiny flowerlets left spoiling in a bowl of stale
water. Did I have to do more?

I answered him with words as well. I reminded him
that we had already lost two good hands to the sweaty
tide of a tempestuous fever. And the iron frames of my
infirmary beds were still as wet and wobbly as a ship's
rail. Because two more took their places and there are
probably others shivering at home who could benefit
from a bed within earshot of the doctor's lively footsteps.
I told him what I meant by epidemic. I left the word on
my tongue and everything else I said had to be forced
around it. I ventured to speculate about the invisible life
of the germ, its way of walking between the steer and the
man who drives it along. Epidemic feeds itself on distance, I said at last. I asked him how far he could see
ahead of his own footsteps.

I wanted to show him my notes, the record of my observations, the list of names that have fallen under my
care. Instead, I drew the hand-size steel stamp from my
pocket, teased its vicious bite with the tip of my finger.
The imprint that its metal teeth could leave on the heavy
bond of the death certificate or the notice of quarantine,
appears as a raised pattern of pustules not unlike the disease that precedes it. Though I opened my palm beneath
Moertle's examining eye—as though I would let the
glinty metal bite his nose—Moertle could only guess how

138

the stamp would leave the same marks on the documents of injunction should they ever be nailed to the slaughterhouse doors. I didn't say another word. I had already dispatched my testimony to the carrier of the mails and it was now an official matter.

"There's no way of telling anything about this one," came the relieved tone in Moertle's voice as he showed me his back.

For myself, I listed this dead steer with the other ones: one stranded in an empty grain cellar, one with its head caught in a broken sewer grate, one collapsed into a dry fountain that spurted only pellets of broken cement into an empty trough when the carcass fell. And for each of them, I took another call to attend the bedside of a man with a swollen foot, one with a bursting tongue, one with fever seeping from his enflamed joints.

Hoof and mouth is a disease of four-legged creatures, but I have crossed the distance between the hot side of the man and the fallen breast of the animal to find them lying in the same place.

Because we begged to hear the rest of the story, the wooden boy sprang from the snapping maw of the suitcase to gain the rhythms of my Papa's bouncy knee.

"A suitcase is for journeys. When you come back there are so many stories to unpack.

"'Your stories do not listen,' was the pealing complaint of the wooden sister to her brother. The rough grain of an unsanded beam showed her feeling where it jutted from her forehead. 'To run away from the woodsman is only to begin to hear the story it will tell in my seashell ears, each morning picking them up from the damp of my sunken pillow. Though the story always leads backward like an open road, yet won't it be always on our backs like a fire, driving us ahead of it as we run.'

"She spoke distractedly, picking splinters from her hair as though they were embers, pinching off the life of the flame that could engulf her wooden self in the time of an indrawn breath."

The boy went right on with his story. He foretold how they would be borne out of darkness beneath the arch of a stone bridge. Under the arch of a high-vaulted stone bridge, they would be two children standing amidst the abandoned bones of trolls, dry but still tufted with meat at the joints. Where giants of time had apparently feasted, brother and sister would discover that they were home.

And looking out from beneath the glowering arch of the bridge they might prick their eyes on needlepoint spires—castles of enchantment—shimmering at last within reach. The black wings of the forest still hanging off their backs could be moulted with a shrug. (For an instant, the wooden sister would see the shadow of one dark feather plummet into the woodsman's pooled gaze.) And as they stepped out from beneath the arched brow of the bridge, the two would join hands across a swiftly running sky. It would be flowing between them over many slippery stones washed in the creek bed where they must travel. They would walk on until they stepped clumsily upon an old woman's face. The flaring mirrors of a cat's eyes would roll upward in her head before she beckoned them onto the dry bank, her reflection vanishing from the oracular surface of water still trickling behind them.

Following the old one up a slope of piled stones, sounding fragile as eggs underfoot, the two young ones would be able to see how everything that hovered above their heads could be pulled down to their level and laid out at their feet. For where the old woman would lead them to the crest of the slope they would see that it was also a fearful precipice. They would tremble, unable to speak, hearing the wind pass between them as through the ribs of a devoured prey. Because they would not be able to make out what was beneath them—the chasm is so deep—they would turn their faces to the sound of the old woman's parting lips.

"What lies below?" she would ask. The children would be so grateful to have no need of the asking themselves. They could release their eyes to the wind whistling over the lip of land and wait blindly for all the valley's depth and the knowledge of everything in it to rise upon the woman's white tongue.

"What lies below is a forest of sounds. But the loudest sound in the forest is the tick tick tick of the woodsman's axe. Though it cuts only one, every tree reverberates with the blows he gives."

The old woman's lips would become the bubble that bursts. "Between one blow and the next no wedge of silence divides the woodsman from his work. The echo from the other trees fills the space of the axehead when it is alternately withdrawn from the heart of the wood. And so nothing is carved out of the quiet distance by the advancing edge of the blade. That is why you seem to hear nothing except my voice, which keeps the woodcutter at his work, pressed by my tongue, food for your ears, but only a bellyful of words."

Then clack clack clack was all that reverberated from the wooden jaw and as though my Papa had forgotten where the voice was coming from, his lips took a tentative grip on the air—eyes shut as an infant nosing after the nipple that floats through the darkness—and only loosened. Even the clacking of the wooden jaw ceased. The children of wood were still as trees. The old woman might have swallowed the head of the axe where the unsuspecting woodsman heaved it thoughtlessly over his shoulder, so silent was the room.

And who was left to say what would happen next but my own clucking self? It was so easy for me to think of the song that the woodcutter was singing and to find the tones of the old woman's voice—delectable to my mouth as a trail of breadcrumbs wagging through the forest—as she would have told it.

So I waited for my brothers and sisters in the outer room, waited for them to drift out as the wave of expectation ebbed, waiting as they were for my Papa to resume, until the tears in his eyes began to overflow the silence and the children began to know that what seemed to be empty was full and left no room for them. And because it was full and left them no room, I waited, certain to catch them by the door with the promise of more.

"There is more to the story than they can tell. There is the song that the woodcutter is singing just to himself without frightening birds out of their trees or scaring the rabbits back into their holes. The song is a mouthful of fur, it is so soft. But really, the song is not much more than a noose on his tongue pulled gently from the darkest hold of his system, and causing the opposite of pain.

"And the song is an anthem of the woodcutter's skill:

142

What is cut from the trees
It's a pity to see,
Puts no fingers or toes on the earth.

For its life is a ruse
That no witness can use,
Except to embellish the truth.

Since I chop down the trees
I confess I'm a tease,
Who has dimpled a log now and then.

But the face that you see
Carved out of the tree
Gives you only the image of men.

"The last line of his song breaks with such force from his lips that the woodcutter misses the mark in the wood. The log underfoot appears to slip because it is the foot that moves in two directions—the toe jumps forward away from the axe, the protruding knuckle of the maimed part flops backward, shivering with rage. But the woodsman doesn't lose his balance.

"The fury in the offended foot kicks back, scattering the toes into a pile of fresh wood chips, the empty boot tip lying like a ruptured pod."

Emptying a pocketful of wood chips—fistfuls of my own mattress filling—into their eager hands, I urge my brothers and sisters to decide which ones could be the tips of the woodcutter's toes.

Having waited until the ground began to suck at his boot heel, my Moertle is convinced that the rain will revive the old prairie in its dead skin of dust.

143

When the rain first came, his was the most skeptical eye that blinked at the sky. He batted the first drops with his eyelashes as though they were tears of embarrassment, and he turned his back on the wet road that has always watered his memory where it leads him home to a dry hole. When the rain stopped as abruptly as it had started, my Moertle alone was unaffected. Having seen it as a taunt from the first and having steeled himself, he was immune from the helpless shudder that lasts long after there has been any contact with the ticklish rib. The others began to feel a dull throb where the joyous finger had poked them.

But then it started raining again and would not stop. Or it would stop only long enough for someone to push a stake into the ground and measure how far it went. Then the rain would resume as though under orders. Watching from their porches or from beneath the opera house awning, those who were old enough began to hold their silent recollections of the green earth inside their mouths like chunks of tobacco soaking up the juices until they could spit. Then they talked impetuously about how it had been before the drought, blurting their memories into the sodden air that fairly rippled around their words.

That is when my Moertle began to wait, not for the rain to end but for the effects to declare themselves unequivocally, like a voice from the clouds. And soft as it was, the earth began to preserve the imprint of everything that passed over it. People could look down to see where they had been.

My Moertle waited until the mud was so slick that a man couldn't stand in his own footsteps without moving. Only then did he fling himself onto the back of the road

144

wriggling toward his home. Now the road is green and glistening and as hard to grasp as the snake in the hole.

But my Moertle knows what to expect, and he is grateful for the struggle uphill, the soft mud drawing his feet so far apart in his stride that he might be the bowlegged range rider himself, galloping home through a blue tide of prairie grass. Because everything is flowing, he is sure that he is moving faster than he ever did before. Just as swiftly as the limp stalks of his legs are swept out from under him by the slippery current of mud, they sprout again, planted firmly, pushing him toward the light.

Back in town, they are turning their heads toward the ominous gurgling of sewers. They are becoming used to leaving their boots at the door. The brims of their Stetsons are falling like wilted petals from the sour lip of the vase, and the incessant drum roll of rain on corrugated tin rooftops is accepted by all as a prelude to rust. Only the men in the slaughterhouse are oblivious to the downpour, since their ears are continuously flushed with the torrential clatter of knives and winch handles and breaking bones.

So my Moertle has abandoned the corral today. Because he is beginning to trust that the cloudy puddles are not receding, that the earth is finally full and beginning to ladle its rich broth over the surface, and that all who step upon it will take a part in molding this clay of creation. That is why he leapt from the fence posts of the corral as though from the rail of a sinking ship, believing that from this moment on there was no difference. He has decided to leap because there is no longer any shore to swim to and though the road he follows measures a certain distance, his arrival home will be as though he were to swallow deeply and sink to the bottom of the thirst he has floated on ever since the rescuers stripped his pale cheek from the parched kiss of the flame and dragged him off his first sea legs, bobbing upon the shock waves of collapsing house beams.

Now, standing on the burbling lip of the old foundation hole, my Moertle need not stoop to greet himself. During the rainy days of his forbearance, his watery self has risen meekly to the surface. This is the meeting my Moertle has anticipated with much patience and a little grief, suspecting all the while that the rain would stop, the image of himself recede in the dank hole, and the rocks bare their teeth once more against his pacing foot when he descends into it. But now he knows he can expect even more.

My Moertle is now prepared to stand still in this place until the leaping grasses can grow to tickle his calves again, all their tongues wagging in a summer's wind and the wind singing with pleasure around the four corners of the house, because taut as it is, stretched over the stiff angles of clapboard construction, the wind is as gentle as a silken cord pulled across the groin. And the white clouds that float behind my Moertle's watery image proffer the first wall of the old clapboard house that he believes must now spring up behind him from such a well-watered plot of land. So that if he can wait long enough for the last shimmering surface tension to ebb from the wavy glass, he will turn from his reflection in the water to behold the very world that cast it there, now hovering where my Moertle has always trusted it to be, enduring beyond the illusory transformations of flickering perception, fixed like the light of shadows forever over his unshrugging shoulder.

146

So, down he goes into the flooded foundation hole, immersing himself, knees and shoulders and head, leaving a scum of air bubbles on the surface like some amphibious roe.

And when his eldest daughter raises her head over the last rise of the uphill road upon which she has tracked him—counting the footsteps as though they were crumbs of bread deposited into the palm of her hand—she is the one to witness his emergence from the destructive element. She cannot see what is holding him below the water line, but she recognizes the unbalanced movements of his upper body as the weakening spasms of a furtive tug of war. Until she draws closer, she cannot see that it is the burden of his own arms and not some demon of the pool that is holding his shirttail under water.

For he is cradling the limp bones of a small calf, brown and white, drenched with the weight of its death and causing him to wobble on his own legs as though he had fallen into someone else's arms, depending on their strength to carry him through. The calf's open eyes are lumps of congealed fat, bulging until they must have disgorged the pupils, black pearls remaining on the muddy bottom. My Moertle might be lifting the dead calf upon a high altar, he is struggling so hard to keep it above water and to get a foothold for himself that will lift him back onto solid ground.

Standing above the water line with the dead calf dripping off his arms, my Moertle confronts his eldest daughter. She is immovable and standing far enough off to break up his view of resurrected pasture land behind her. Her resolute bearing casts a ragged shadow on the sparkling steps of the new porch where my Moertle's hopes sit waiting. She flounces. She might be poised to turn on the step and enter the house by herself. The whole house trembles under her shadowy touch. My Moertle is no longer certain that the steps will bear his weight as well. And his feet begin to pace nervously under the balanced weight of his immobilized head and shoulders. He wants to ask her to move, but she does not appear willing to answer.

The calf must have lowered its face to drink too close to the edge of the pool and when the soft lip gave way under two hooves, the animal fell through the sky as quickly as the passing of a breath over water. Unless it was a dog.

Now the sky is steady in the unblinking eye of the pool. And now my Moertle's back lies as flat on the reflective surface as the shadow that has fallen between himself and his unflinching daughter.

MONOLOGUE OF THE SPOTTED DOG

Into the pool, I follow my master. I am the crust of bread washed under a tankard splash of heady brew. The water closes over me. My ears are gulping, my eyes are lips for the passage of liquid. They have never been anything else but wet. That is what my master loved about me. He could see himself there, a pale stick of a man dipped into a sticky depth. Now it is his own depth swimming to me.

Moertle has asked me for my prognosis: not merely the word that will pronounce Lilli's fate but the story it

will tell in all the slow footsteps of its progress. Moertle
can no longer sit patiently beside Lilli's bedpost essaying
the discipline of the sickroom watch. Instead, he circles
round the outside of the boardinghouse—bare-headed,
bent forward, hands joined behind his back, alternately
washed with rain and sunlight—giving a circumference
to the disease that turns as palpably as the earth on its
axis and might, he believes, advance the clock on Lilli's
fate. Just so, he might see the outcome before it has whittled him away with all the meticulous attention of waiting for the bladed arm of the clock to fall.

But I am now in a position to unfold the tale of this
infection because the pattern has repeated itself con-
clusively on all of the pages of my notebook. It now contains only a single pinch of salt-white pages at the back. I
could tear them out and toss them over my shoulder with
confidence that there will be no new developments.

Though I cannot repeat too often that hoof and mouth
is a disease of four-legged creatures, I am not mistaken in
my diagnosis. And to make it plain to him, I offer Moertle the analogy with the slaughterhouse where he works.

The protocol of symptoms: first, there is the sensation of heat that crowds the body in its routine movements as though the skin were ample enough to
accommodate more than one person at a time. Inflamma-
tion of the joints accounts for this. But the bruised sensation that calls massaging fingers directly to knees and
elbows comes later. I needn't add that the course of the
disease is indirection.

When the sensations of heat and swelling have been
herded into the very center of the patient's palpitating
chest, a sudden fever abandons all unpleasant sensations

149

like a hot-air balloon loosed from its mooring into a delirium of blue sky. And because the patient's distraction is great, changes may occur at ground level that go unnoticed until the carcass has been dragged so far off its conscious bearings that even the subtlest awareness of that distance, like the briefest glance down from a precipice, brings the dizzy mind to a crashing encounter with itself. But, by this time, the arms and legs are limp. The feet in particular have become as soft as hands though they can get no grip on the things of this earth. The swelling is greatest in the armpits and at the tops of the thighs, bulging pockets of flesh, where an intermittent, knifing pain releases a hot salt sea of sensation that would arouse an angry rash on any other part of the body.

And the tongue lolls helplessly in the mouth because the severed head of the patient's awareness has once again rolled out of reach of the flailing body. The fever recurs with greater frequency, and the body shrinks in proportion to the expanding air that heats it. And it is this heat that draws the fluids from the inner organs until they are nothing so much as a cluster of sticky raisins that would fall together in the dust.

On this, the final threshold of the body's fervid metamorphosis, deprived of limbs and head and the tail that carries the spark between them, the patient hangs on the hooked finger of death like the sweetest batter to be licked.

As I expected, Moertle exclaims upon the resemblance to the side of beef and most particularly the hook that carries the patient off. But he wants to note one point of radical divergence between the slaughterhouse haunch and the woman who lies beneath us now. The woman's belly does not shrink before the swinging scythe of her fever. He urges that I resist the temptation of simplistic analogy. He states that too often well-observed resemblances are mistaken for identity: the difference, he says, is that this woman will bear fruit in the tropical fever of her delirium. He is aware that the birds of the perspiring jungle hatch the colors of the most enflamed sky in their damp nests. The tropical monkeys bear fur that is already singed with the sun dilated in their simmering eyes, and the snakes bear a balm against the sun in their own blood that chills the eggs when they tremble upon life. So, he wonders, will Lilli's baby be born a creature of the jungle or will it bear the imprint of the hoof that kicked her here?

I ask him why he cares so little for the child's life.

I know he cannot answer. The cowl of silence shielding his face gives him a cloistered look. He might as well be a shadow flickering at the far end of an arched stone tunnel. But he is standing stoop-shouldered beside me, his breath coming like footsteps down the length of the tunnel. I place my hand on his back. The breathing is soothed, the back and head are raised from the prayerful attitude of his stoop. The face lifts, brightens, and I can feel the pressure of my hand making a levered speech between his shoulder blades.

Moertle blurts his horror of the infant's face. He would place coins in the eyes at birth to block the light from its eyes, to arrest its movements, which are too noisy and wild. He would have to tie the pink-budded hands and feet, making the tiny body smaller and smaller with each tightening of the knots, confining its movements like a fly in a jam jar. Then he would carry the jar high under one arm, drift out into the air of a blustery morning, let the wind draw him to a blue precipice, where, unscrewing the jar, he would take the most ecstatic relief from the slow sucking sound that smothers the hectic buzz at its release.

Or so he seems to say, as I watch him struggle with awkward lips for the words.

My Moertle circles the boardinghouse, unable to tell the first step of each orbit from the last. His grey Stetson is all that is visible from the upper story, where Lilli breathes laboriously for two. The weight of her stomach holds her flat to the bed as though the fetus were sitting up on her and weighing with all the years of maturity already accumulated like water in the bulging sac of its life. Each day my Moertle lays his open palm against the expanding skin of the mother's belly, feeling for the floating shape of the head, nub of a finger, kissing cheek of one buttock, kick of hoof, or point of horn. He is afraid to probe deeper with the finger that lifts and scratches his own head, unless he should burst the sac.

A declivity in the crown of my Moertle's wide-brimmed Stetson holds a thimbleful of rainwater that winks at the children where they are peering down on him. There is nothing for them to see in their mother's eyes, which are shut. And they are not permitted to stand beside their father when he draws the covers back, clutching the stiff floor lamp to the bedside. During the father's examination, the children must sit in their separate rooms. They will exert their patience until the weight of my Moertle descending the stairs rattles the staircase to the ground,

signaling them to return to the window to resume counting the orbits of his vigil below.

But today it is the weight of the doctor, enough for
two men, that sends shivers through the floor, calling the
children inadvertently to witness my Moertle in bed with
his wife.

Frozen in their father's blue stare, each child experiences the paradoxical melting of nerve where the hot recognition gleams through them like a tungsten filament.

Sitting up in bed, bareheaded, my Moertle suddenly
must balance his attention between the protruding face of
children—against which he is forcing the firm hand of his
grimace—and the bulbous anatomy of the woman, where
his fingers are attached and sparking convulsions that
wires couldn't conduct without bursting into flames.

Such is the force that the bed taps its metal feet against
the floor, as though its legs were jointed and limber.

The voltage of this shock runs through my Moertle like
mice over a roomful of bare feet. But the high-pitched
shriek belongs to the children who have been engorged
into one mouth of fright. There is nothing in my Moertle's mouth. Nothing at all for him to bite down on, to
submerge the trauma that is so evident in the hairs rearing up on his head, the heat streaming from his nostrils.

For he cannot stop the voice. Though his lips are still,
the voice is moving through him with the involuntary life
of a convulsion. And the children, whose eyes have already met the maddening eyes—someone has garishly
painted them under the naked brow of their mother's
belly—have already guessed that the secret mouth of the
belly is caught and struggling between my Moertle's fingertips. For the hand that is not free and fumbling with

the specter of intruding children is plunged between their mother's legs. From that mouth or any other the children would have recognized the voice of the wooden doll.

They hear the voice but they cannot listen. Neither can they speak. The breeze through the open door behind them no longer whispers escape. All the air is stilled to a held breath. And now the room is sealed up in one sensation of heat and light, throbbing with four words that, as they become audible, seem to be stamping irate feet against the collapsing walls of the children's hearing.

". . . children . . . never . . . grow . . . old . . ."

My Papa brings me the dog in the arms of a lullabye. His lips move inaudibly but I know the words. And each word causes a silent reflex movement of my tongue as though people were stepping upon a loose floorboard to get to my thoughts.

But I cannot fathom the expression on my Papa's face, which is wet and dripping as the lifeless hide of the dog. The carcass lies across my Papa's outstretched arms. The legs are long and limp as river grass bent in a steady current. The tongue alone might be alive. It starts violently from the twisted jaw. It is a muscular fist flexed with pent-up action, but it is clenched between immovable teeth and might be already severed in their grip.

My Papa does not see this. His sight is blurred but I cannot tell if the water in his eyes flows from the dark pool still swirling in his trouser cuffs—the pool is behind him—or from some deeper reservoir within. If he is drenched in his own grief, he may never be wrung dry.

When he sees me, his outstretched arms reach

painstakingly further as though he would deposit his burden with me, or as though he would take me up into his arms as well and make his burden greater. I wave him off. For I have come to reveal the futility of his concern. Today I have a reason for making myself visible, for leaping from the shadows of stealth into the prickly glare of my Papa's consciousness. So now, staring into the face of my Papa's preoccupation—and because it has pointed ears and a tail—I am happy to tell him that he is no longer enthralled, that the cattle trains have been halted—all the wetted machinery is stilled, signs have been posted—that the slaughterhouse is closed.

I tell him that the corrals are already stagnant with puddles of disinfectant. And from within the corrugated walls of the main building, only the sound of the snakepit is audible, because they are spraying. Every square inch of floor, walls, and ceiling, of gleaming blades or bruised rubber conveyer belt, every expanse of cutting board must be shed of its surface area replaced by the slithering chemical skin. It has a venomous sting if it gets under the worker's skin.

But my Papa doesn't understand. His lips have not ceased their silent music. He is standing close enough so that his shadow makes a bridge between us. With one foot poised in front, he seems to be testing the strength of the bridge, only to retreat into the stalwart posture without which the dead animal would thud to the ground. It appears that he will never be able to move from the spot and that the music will never cease to flow from his lips—nor will it ever be audible unless there is a listener herself already possessed of the words.

CLOSED BY ORDER OF COUNTY CORONER

A pestilence is upon this place.

Walk upon these premises and you will be cloaked in the skin of contagion that is no epidermis. Breathe the air and become the priest of its communion, spreading its pollen with every word you speak. The grounds are no less hazardous than the enclosed places. Because in this season the grounds are always wet and running, their resemblance to the open sores of proverb has particular virulence.

Therefore let no finger be improperly placed. Tread lightly in your retreat. Take every breath with caution. Stifle the appetite of the lungs: in order to save them, empty them. Instead, fill your quickening stride with the evasive twists and turns of the dance-hall contortionist, that the rainment of infection may not rest too long on any single part of your anatomy.

And when you think you are safely delivered from the heaving loins of contamination, take extra precautions that you do not inadvertently become its lethal spawn.

Wash inside and out.

The skin can stand the most bristling assault of the scrub brush. Remember, each pore is a cavity, a puckering sac that would suckle the life of the orphaned germ. So, make each pore reflect the firelight of cleanliness from the back of the cave no matter how it burns.

As for the internal organs, follow the rites of emetic. Do not negotiate with the tongue for the most congenial tastes, but let its spasmodic revulsions be a cue and a catalyst to all the organs that are connected with it by the porous telepathy of visceral tissue, all of which must bubble and boil and flutter with dry heaves like a sheet in the wind, before you may be confident of purgation.

Let the bowels be evacuated.

Let your nail parings be burned in a palm-sized declivity of earth.

Make a pyre of your clothes.

The hairs of the scalp will grow back.

Finally, take a place in the sun where the sweat of these exertions may evaporate into the arms of an expansive wind. Sit calmly. Loosen the girdle of all physical bearing. Do not let even your thoughts wander in the direction of these corrals, and you may preserve yourself at last from the salty corrosion of the fever blister.

Who is strong enough for such forbearance?

Dr. Hugo Face

When he reads this, my Moertle resolves to set up the corral around the walls of the boardinghouse by walking in circles. A corral is a perimeter after all, he says to himself. As such, it is the means by which every man will give a center to his thoughts. Our weakness, he confesses, is that being capable of such careful delimitation, no man is content to sit on the perimeter of his world merely counting his stock, taking confidence from the enclosure of his own mind. No. The life at the center of his thoughts gives such amorous looks that he is at last drawn into it. He leaps from the fence rail. He strides toward the center, only to realize with the first twinge of irrevocability unwrinkling like the impress of the fence rail in the seat of his pants, that without the perimeter there is no center—unless it remains dilating in the steadier eye of someone who watched you make your move, the one who was there beside you and who is still sitting on the fence rail with a smile breaking his face into pieces.

157

Moertle's orbit has finally closed around the sickbed where the first birth tremors stir the patient without waking her. The doctor's hands, encased in rubber, are flexing ready for any emergency. But he predicts a normal birth, except that the mother will be oblivious to its occurrence. Because her consciousness does not lurk beneath her fallen eyelids—he searches one last time between his rubber fingertips where the eye is spread—the doctor informs Moertle that he must take her place, supplying the motion of the spirit there, where the buoyant motion of the mother's breast will supply the body.

But Moertle protests—fingers curling back toward his face and the face quivering like a loose mask—that he will not handle the child.

The doctor admonishes him: "It is a winding road that you would follow if you were to discover where she is gone. And then you would have to bring her back."

"Dinah the Damsel in Distress" dances mouse steps over the stage to convey the impression of a swift and uneventful journey. The train of her gown sweeps a cloud of dust in her trail. The rest of the stage is dark and ominous with the sound of bass drums building invisible thunderheads in the flies. And it is unclear to the audience whether her song is the alarum of flight or the battle cry of pursuit.

Only when she begins to ascend inexplicably into the air does the audience realize that, in her mincing passage across the stage, she has been climbing a pantomime staircase of stone steps, each wound one above the other like the threads of a coiling rope lowered into a well. But it is meant to be a tower as tall as the well is deep that she is climbing. And

158

though now the audience can plainly see that she is rising on a wooden platform edged with the papier-mâché battlements of the tower, it is indeed all swaying precariously on four invisible ropes.

Mario! Mario! Mario! . . .

The sequined front of her gown glitters with tears and her arms are moving as though she could pluck the tears from her breast, flinging the jewels to her lover who is circling below.

The bed is alive with the intimations of a thrashing infant already violently spinning the cocoon of its first tantrum, though the mother lies still and dormant in the hectic life of the bedsprings. And so the patient resembles the prisoner stretched on the rack where she has been beaten senseless—her arms pulled to the headboard and knotted there, her legs tied astride of the mattress at points bisecting the length of the frame to keep them canted and splayed. And in this way the rattling of the bed frame conveys a resonant echo of the torturer's blows.

The doctor himself pockets the unused lengths of rope.

On the bed's opposite flank Moertle is stranded. He is unable to cross to the doctor's side because to pass the foot of the bed would mean to stand for a flickering instant between the woman's open legs and so to be cast in the leaping shadow of the womb. Therefore he implores the doctor to cross to his side for a better view of the patient's labors. Though Lilli's body is displayed beneath them both, as taut and revealing as a pinned map waiting only for the guiding finger to trace its secret ways, Moertle protests that the patient's condition can be more truthfully read from movements occurring beneath the

159

skin, provided no one lays a finger upon the pulse of that life.

But the doctor already thinks he sees the infant's head and eagerly extends his hands as though to seize a weight that he could lay upon Moertle's tongue.

Though the ropes supporting the platform are supposed to erect the illusion of the high tower, the slowness of the ascent more vividly evokes the weight of the woman standing upon it. Backstage, the hand at the winch has begun to shed real tears. Each turn of the handle produces a more inflexible tension in the stagehand's shoulders and a more violent motion of the wooden platform. But just when the audience perceives an unsteadiness in the voice to match the derelict sway of the wooden gondola—and they appreciate the dangerous height from which the song falls to the ears—the upward motion ceases. The tower is fully erected. The song is on steady legs again. Except that the song ceases, too. And though the ropes that support each corner of the wooden gondola are relieved of their motion, the audience now observes that there are ropes attached at the shoulders and hem of the heroine's glittery black gown and these are still moving. "Dinah the Damsel in Distress" is finally the puppet trying to free herself from the wicked entanglement of her strings. As it rises, the audience can see that the hem of the gown is a second curtain over the stage. Though it requires a more squinty eye—it is so close to the lights that shine from the catwalks—the gaze it commands is no less expectant than if it were waiting upon a courtyard of royal actors.

The doctor's face is bowed between Lilli's legs as though he could whisper to the child to come, bearing it away as easily as one takes a kiss from affectionate lips. The doctor can preserve the air of intimacy because his

160

hands, placed atop the patient's belly, are exerting their wordless pressure. He is holding her down, putting all of his weight, heavy as the stone at the mouth of a windy cavern, upon that part of her anatomy most predisposed to roll away. For the contractions have begun.

Because the patient sleeps still in the hollow depths of her body, the first contractions come to the surface on the fingertips of a demonic puppeteer, making the wooden foot dance, the painted hand wave. The eyes flash open and shut, seeing nothing. But because the doctor controls her center of gravity, Lilli will not involuntarily fling herself off the bed. And while Moertle has stepped back in anticipation of just such a calamity, he is no longer shielding his gaze against it. Seeing that the doctor may not be able to restrain the patient much longer, Moertle says nothing. He does nothing. For Moertle has seen a man kicked by a bull in the corral, and he has noticed that the most violent motion knows no restraint whatsoever, unless it is the very stretch of the muscle it is tied to.

That is why Moertle has his own vision of things. And now because Moertle's gaze is already bumped by the spectacle of the doctor losing his balance, losing his grip on the patient, and because Moertle's concentrating eye is already asplash with the thrashing arms and legs of the doctor's unmoored and drowning self, he has to wipe a droplet from his eye. Whether it is wrung from hilarity or terror, he cannot guess. But judging from the depth to which he has been shaken, Moertle quietly reaffirms his conviction that the expected child will be born unexpectedly with a hoof or a horn. One way or another it is a day for being tossed out of the corral.

But the doctor had not been bucked from the flanks of Lilli's womb. Nor has he lapsed from his perfect control of the mother's convulsing anatomy. And if his hands are suddenly drenched with the intensity of Moertle's vision, it is because, as he says with momentous calm, the mother's water has broken.

When the black hem of the gown has risen to her midriff, the light struck between Dinah's legs like a blade to part them, glints the fire of tempered steel nowhere brighter than where it reveals the skintight fit of the silver lamé leotard. It is as alive beneath the wide bell of the dress as though it were grabbing her for her life. And the still rising hem of the gown receives its broken reflection from the metallic and mirroring cells of her emerging body—flashing waist, winking midriff and peering breasts—just before disappearing into the flies like soot off a flame. When she is completely free of the gathering nimbus and the gown has vanished altogether—she has by now taken two of the rope supports into her hands, lifting one then the other foot onto the swaying papier-mâché parapet—she stands atop the stone tower in the attitude of one who will certainly jump or fly.

So it comes as a relief to the audience when, from out of the wings stage left, the spread-eagle form of the naked flier is met by the swinging bar of the circus trapeze. In one graceful movement, she manages to catch herself in midair, point her toes at the stage floor, lift and roll herself inside out until she is sitting where her own hands snatched her from the maw of gravity.

Opposite this breezy perch and as high above the stage as she now sits, the stone parapet still sways on its four ropes, echoing the force with which Dinah kicked herself off into the thin air.

But from where she is looking down on the audience, the

lights are so close she can no longer distinguish the hot breath roaring inside her skull from the halo of brightness she is forced to put on when she raised herself into position for her finale. The sensation is as unequivocal as it is unexpected. Though her feet have replaced her hands on the bar and her upright stance is carefully balanced against the sway of the trapeze, the feverish pulse at her temples is tipping her backward, throwing her off the rhythms of her performance as forcefully as though it possessed shoulders and arms to work its will upon her.

And now she must relinquish one rope support in order to receive her baton from the flyspace lofted above her head, which is cut off from the audience's view by a ruffled curtain. Before her hand has reached the hem of the curtain and high enough to grasp its prize, it dips back into view to catch her balance on the rope and so miss the baton as it falls, nearly striking her head before the hand's own reflex can recover its purpose.

Then, with the baton lifted in one hand, "Dinah the Damsel in Distress" resumes the graceful motion of a theatrical bow, lifting one foot off the trapeze bar, bending it behind her, dipping her head into the brass fanfare on the stage as though she would sip from the effervescent bell of the tuba, toasting the performance to come. Though she is about to strike the spark that will ignite the baton, she experiences a premature flash of heat across her face as though she were already consumed in the flame. And the performance begins.

The infant's head floats between the doctor's hands, confusing the sensation of his own strength with the buoyancy of awakening life. But just when it seems that the tide of the amniotic sac should flush the walls of the womb and deliver the child like a fish from a fresh wave, the flow abruptly ceases and the infant's narrow shoulders are twisted in a dry pucker of lips that will not permit another word.

The startling growth of hair on the infant's head sponges perspiration from the doctor's hands where he refuses to give up his grip on the delivery. He plants his elbow more firmly in the mattress and at an angle for leverage. He spreads his knees upon the floor for a more powerful grip than he could get with his feet. The heave of the mattress against his chest gives him the illusion of his own breasts when he throbs against it. He is forced to thrust his hips out behind him in order to have a counter-weight against the maternal belly.

In this ambiguous posture of desire, the doctor casts a sideways glance at his companion, but Moertle will not oblige with hand or word to help.

And though Moertle's attention is clenched in the grip of Lilli's canted hips as tightly as the infant's squinting brow, he sticks there with the knowledge of protruding horn or hoof—unimaginable in the doctor's lore of anat-omy—which has surely snagged a few silken threads of the uterus walls, unraveling the tapestry of the minotaur entangled in the pathways of escape. For Moertle per-ceives this complication as a portent of all the expanding life that must prove incompatible with the contractions of the body, though he cannot control his impulse to clasp the mystery beneath the trembling lids of his own eyes.

But if he should open them now, he would see how the muscles in the doctor's wrists are flexing so close to the infant's temples that they might be attached at the skull and throbbing some ingenious telepathy that could help soften the knot in the mother's belly. For it is with a shiver of burst threads that the lips of the womb finally relax their grip. And the infant anatomy is propelled into the doctor's recoiling hands on a thrusting tongue of inertia that leaves it pink and glistening as candy that melts in the mouth. Moertle would be the first to see how perfect is the physical form of the newborn child. Hands and feet, all an accomplished mimicry of the human, would make Moertle wonder what he could have expected.

The baton burns at both ends in the performer's hand of grace. "Dinah the Damsel in Distress" can twirl a canopy of sparks over her head or thread the sinews of flame through her kicking legs with lariat swiftness. But for this performance she has added the extra challenge of the trapeze. And because she has added to the erratic movement of the flame the unsteadiness of the ground below, the audience may not detect a subtle flickering of her nerve.

For though she holds the fiery baton at arm's length, Dinah begins to believe that she may not elude the sparks jumping to her head. Because there and just behind her eyes an ember of fever already breathes a redder heat with every pendulum swing of the trapeze bar, and what spits and darts at the end of the baton seems to touch the tongue of her own worst fears each time her gaze slips to the ground.

For now is the moment of her most defiant nimbleness. Because the dancer's knees are strung to the reflexes of a practice regimen, she flexes, without thinking, the postures of greatest risk. The knees give way to a bodily crouch almost low enough to touch her sequined belly to the bar. With her arms outstretched on either side, the nearness of her center of gravity to the axis of the bar is all that balances her in midair. And just when it appears she cannot make herself flatter to the bar, she tips heels over head as though to flatten herself on the stage below.

Now all can see that the motion of her body forward was propelled by the motion of her feet in the opposite direction. And where her ankles have gained a purchase in the angles of rope and bar she has taken a new perch upon which she can now slowly straighten her legs and stand up in the inverted space of the proscenium. Now, standing beneath the bar and upside down, she is the mirror image of her former self, and her whole body is rippling in the air of suspense as though she had glanced into a trembling pool of darkness.

Raised above her head, the fist clenching the fiery baton dangles thirty feet above the stage. Though her head hangs down yet, the flame still jumps up to the straight ends of her hair whispering its threat of immolation. The audience only waits for the music to set up a buoyant rhythm that might break her fall or douse a conflagration.

Silence. Only the smallest bones of the performer's wrist are in motion, calculating the most particular mechanics of the feat she is about to perform.

Then, suddenly she snaps her wrist and shakes out the whole intricate length of the performance with whiplike accuracy and violence. She watches from the depth of her concentration as the baton twirls end over end far above her until, having attained exactly the calibrated height, it arcs and begins to fall back between the two ropes from which the trapeze and her own elongated self are suspended. It is not merely the paradox of inverse height achieved with the measured motion of her wrist but the parabolic symmetry of the arc describing the baton's descent that causes the audience to gaze with speechless approval as the performer calmly extends one straight arm out behind her and, with perfect confidence, closes her eyes to receive the baton in the partner of the hand that tossed it.

Only a handful of sparks rewards this gesture with the light of revelation.

Because all eyes were gathered expectantly in the palm of the performer's hand, no one saw how far off the mark the glittering shaft of the baton must have fallen to land amiss. And because the violent recoil of the burned hand shook the length of the performer's body to the ropes and more violently shook the ropes to their moorings, no one could say whether she was lowered on emergency turns of the crank handle or whether her abrupt appearance on the stage floor was merely the unrehearsed fatalism of the snapped rope. Finally, because the fire in the performer's hand was the main distraction, no one observed until it was too late that at the top of its beautiful arc a few sparks from the baton must have sailed high enough to catch the curtain riser and there, breathing in all the hovering vastness of the upper stage, must have exhaled the fireball that now radiates upon performer and audience alike the heat of an exploding furnace.

And Moertle is the first to exclaim the miracle of anatomical fitness, the infant hand, the infant foot, shaped to the image of another perfect shape: the hand, the foot turned brusquely upon a sheet of bone-white paper, shot with identifying darts and threaded on the umbilical convolutions of medical names—enticement, entanglement of the life and the chart of the human.

But the new mother is not a match for the colors of the medical chart. She is only another grey patch in the shifting shadows that are rearranging the room with the recklessness of changeable weather. And for the two men, nodding their heads over the fallen mound, the spectacle of Lilli's physical collapse is little more than the empty footprint of a passage that might well have shaken the earth, but passed too quickly to imprint the memory with a shadow shape. Their interest lies with the living. The two men move closer to one another as though certain signs had passed between them, though it is only the meaty sides of their bodies that have communicated. And when Moertle's face hovers closely enough over the cradle of the doctor's swaying hands, the medical practitioner rudely withdraws the offering.

He will not solicit another opinion. He steps back to show Moertle a frown. But Moertle sees only that it is a threat drowned in perspiration and suffused with a heat rash. He observes the loosening edges of the mask and the steam escaping from the receding eyes. Feverishly exchanging one hand for the other beneath the infant's roiling back, the doctor delivers his last prognosis.

The child will not live. In all the infinitesimal spaces of its labyrinthine creation, the spark of the mother's fever has already flared. The doctor attests to its scorching breath on the open palms of his hands. And the convulsive silences of the infant's tantrum give certain confirmation of how quickly its life is evaporating at the lip of the cauldron.

Moertle's gaze is transfixed by the clacking mouth of the infant rage, struggling to sound but engorged with a livid silence around which no breath can be drawn. The dilated silence, small and red as the teat that might have succored it, brings to Moertle a recognition as mysterious and as terrifying as the one quivering pink eye of the rabbit that stares, oblivious to the existence of the eye on the other side of its head. Once the rabbit looked at Moertle from a patch of waving grass and then the rabbit was gone, until he turned his head and the rabbit was there.

And was it not a baby?

My Moertle swears that the baby never cried. It only sucked air in to feed the flame that had sparked its life until the body became light as ash. It became so slight a burden that the doctor feared he might never feel as though he had shaken it off. Though his arms were empty, he would never escape some sooty entanglement with the air, conjuring smoke to his tearful eyes. He uses the words "contagion, epidemic, quarantine" to express himself.

But my Moertle ignores the passing shadow of the doctor's admonition in order to contemplate the first forming resemblance between the mother and child. They now lie face to face in the only configuration that could accommodate them both to the same box. And because the child shares the space that was considered only big enough for the mother's head, my Moertle can begin to speculate how the child is the oracular condensation of the mother's last breath, last eddy of smoke off the fire, curling into the palpable shape of prophecy and proferred expressly for him to speak about, though he cannot think what to say.

My Moertle inserts a hand between the two cheeks of mother and child and it is like delving into the cool ectoplasm of a mirror, so alike are the sensations he feels on either side. Holding his own breath for buoyancy against that depth, he feels for the bottom of the box. He wishes to know how hard their rest will be. But when he withdraws his hand from its accomplished purpose, he can no longer disguise to himself the more furtive meaning of the gesture, which has permitted him to gather the sensations of one side of the hand and the other into a single membraneous thrill of tactile certainty.

"And was it not a baby?" My Moertle has begun to understand how ambiguous are the symptoms of disease when what appears as one is revealed to be two. And everything must be counted twice when the diagnostic hand moving halfway up the arm discovers a watery lump, when the lips passed over a forehead are made slick enough to swallow, when the foot no longer fits the shoe it wore yesterday. The healer's hand does not cease to transfigure what it touches.

When "Dinah the Damsel in Distress" is carried out beneath the exploding beams of the opera house, my Papa assures himself that it was not the fire that struck her down. It was the fever that felled her from her kindling perch. And though she was plucked from the flame before it could lick her face dry, before it could take her bones between two pulverizing fingers of heat, she has nonetheless been looted by covetous hands of catastrophe, which will never give back a breath, a heartbeat, a flicker of muscle or any echo of life to all the intact hollows of her physical poise. Because she is dead. So my Papa will not step closer to the figure in effigy, where they have laid her upon the flatbed of a nearby truck—parked in awe of the conflagration—because he does not need eyes to see what has occured.

My Papa declaims out loud that she is the puppet cut from her strings. Her arms and legs are bent in the angles of the compressed accordion bellows. The song is still caught between her teeth. And though she is sprawled in the attitude of mortal grief from which she has arisen so many times into the halo of a stage light, my Papa knows she will never again be raised by a few musical notes like thread through a dozen beads. Because my Papa surmises that the third vertebra has been extracted like a stubborn molar from the base of her neck and now moistens the palm of the hand that formerly held the strings.

Lacking sufficient water pressure, the streets have never been equipped with hydrants. The three members of the fire brigade who still remember their duty have come bearing only laborious witness, since they are too inexperienced to disentangle hoses from the racks of an engine long since stripped of wheels and siren. One, prescient enough to bring a bucket, is able to convert it into a seat by emptying its contents on an ember thrown into the street, like a germ from the pod of contagion.

So the fire is attended only by an array of upturned faces, most of which scattered from the auditorium only to recompose themselves on the outside and in rows as regular as the aisle seats, in order to achieve the best view possible of what is certain to climax in utter destruction.

Shivering in its flames, the opera house stands out against the darkened street as though it were gathering inertia for a predatory leap. But the flames, that have already attained the roof, signal its collapse from within, where it is already a molten center, all flowing curtains, plush seat backs, swaying backdrops, piled sandbags, rendered transparent in the moment of their incineration, so that the space of destruction will be violently contracted to the single plane of the eye that beholds it—if any eye could absorb such a concussion that has the force of a bullet. Those on the outside peer through the glare of burst windows spraying dangerous shards of their vision back at them. But it is the heat, not the brightness, of the

171

pyre that has the greatest impact on the audience, that now contains my Papa as a voice in an ectoplasmic aura. The heat sweats them into a paste, congealing closer and closer to the dry mouth of the flame, and my Papa has become indistinguishable amidst the crowding heads. In each of them the darkness of the street has fused with the glow of the fire to create an unsteady motion like the settling of a bed of coals. Yet his words are unmistakable in my ears.

He exhorts over the crowd that they cannot tell the fever from the fire. It has fallen to my Papa to say that the feverish brow produces changes in the world that go unnoticed because they do not leap from the surface of the skin into the third dimension—except as the tensile globules of perspiration from which the world itself bursts whole when they are thrown off from the orbit of sickbed grogginess.

My Papa protests that "Dinah the Damsel in Distress" ignited at a feverish pitch. All who stand in the vaporous illumination of the night will experience that fever only as the pulse of the fire on their faces. They know nothing of the life it dissimulates to their own blood and are forgetful of the differences.

The life of the daughter is indistinguishable from the mother's life when it passed through the broken cage of my fingers. From the day this daughter's shoes began to clutch at her feet when she tried to remove them, her case was out of my hands.

Yet I could not restrain myself from falling into step behind her and down the pathways of a remorseless deterioration that, I soon learned, was for her only the ruthless pursuit of her father's footsteps. A child's pace is bird food for a girth like mine and this young daughter was small enough that I might have carried her whole inside my own belly, no less comfortably than a nourishing dinner. Her search for her papa was a tireless treadmill that in the end rendered me even fitter to comment on the cellular contortions of the disease in all the steps of its advance.

For I knew that the child was already as good as fatherless. Her father's tracks were so confused—by the inky wash of soot from indestructible beams, coagulation of char and kicked-up earth, smoky impregnation of rainwater drained and pooled in so many reflecting ash pits— that no single sense would be able to distinguish what had passed through the scene of fiery devastation from what has stood forever in the same place. And because she did not know where to look, she was forced to look everywhere.

For me, the path was clearer, emblazoned with all the predictable signs. The child's body is more resilient than the adult's, but it maps a smaller territory of invasion for disease. From the moment the child looked up beneath the vacant window of the boardinghouse, I could see that much more than the heat of the sun boiled up on the buttery goose flesh of her brow. I saw that this was the precarious weight she would have to balance on her head all the way to the top of her father's long hill—a road once sharply etched, now blurred by the wash of heavy rains and the sour overflowing of stagnant pools at its destination. I saw how each laborious step would be a hand thrust out of darkness to topple her burden. And at

173

the end of the road I did not miss the minute ache in this pilgrim's flinching joints. They must have been biting her all along the way, like a hive of lice sunk within each socket of bone and cartilage. I counted each faltering step. I felt her welts reddening under my clucking tongue.

All alone at the top of the rise, her searching gaze overflowed with the empty distance that surrounded her. She stooped on the brimming lip of the old foundation hole for company or to peer more sternly beneath the surface, where her loneliness lay undisguised except as the muddy gills of a few bubbling shadows. Seeing her rise, any other witness might have assumed that she had sunk to the depth she contemplated, she was so slow to surface. But I knew that her slowness was merely the heavy stones beginning to pile up against all the skeletal levers of her resilience. The force of gravity was slipping off center inside of her, running to odd corners of her anatomy like sand from the bags that have propped up the most vivid scenery until everything topples forward, immovable in the new places. I might have sacrificed my anonymity then and stepped out from behind the shielding distance that I held between us, in order to conduct my official examination. But there could be no cure. I followed her all the way back until she was forced to walk on the sides of her feet in order to continue a straight path. If the street was narrow she could lean against a flaking wall, but when her search took her out from under the protective shadow of a standing wall, she had to kneel and let her head shiver between her knees until her breath could return to its steady pace.

I could talk to myself as I recorded my observations

174

like the most contented passenger aboard the long train of my pursuit. But she was sworn to speak to no one until she could drink from her Papa's shadow again and so soften her words. What she had to say she held inside the suffering heart of herself like the bruised blood swelling where it beats out the rhythms of a dull pulse.

When she had traveled the circumference of her Papa's longing, she came back to the center. The boardinghouse stood as she had left it, tall, gaunt, its shadow a scolding finger in the street above which the clouds passed impatiently across the face of the sun. And no one is home. The front door lolls open on the porch. The loose steps leading up to the porch have been put awry by a clumsy foot. The weight of this wayward daughter's climbing self is not nearly enough to set the boards back in their proper places. And even though all of her gravity is sagging in the saddle of her back, because now she is crawling on all fours to her destination, she is lighter than when she left. It is the effect of fever.

Inside the front door, staring up as if from the bottom of a dank feed trough, Myrtle contemplates the way up. The staircase rears up four stories that could crush her under the clattering fall of its steps. In the silence of the abandoned hallway, she can already hear the sound of herself tumbling backward from the precipice of her own throbbing temples, where the atmosphere of dread is being turned to sweat and falling from the air like a precipitation of her thoughts. This too is the effect of fever.

And the topmost step is not the last thought prodding this suffering daughter's irritability like a long stick. The slipping rope of her stamina is clearly fastened upon an objective that she will not give up. And so I can see that she will need to thrust herself headlong into the hallway from the landing and with the force she would use to push someone off a mountaintop, if she will reach her mother's bed with the fewest crawling exertions.

Though the bedclothes have been taken as swaddling for the mother's grave, the stripped mattress bears the patient's vivid imprint as clearly as marks in stone. And as the intaglio seems to give birth to the stone, so the dead-fall of this daughter's body into her mother's bed brings the mattress to life with a sudden motion and a cry of sprung metal. What appeared at first to be merely the shivering reverberations of her collapse appears now to be a deliberate violence and ghostly pantomime of the upheavals of the mother's labor.

For having found the impress of serrated vertebrae cleaving the center of the mattress, having nested herself so to speak in the wet fishbone hairs of her mother's nervous system, Myrtle is racked by jolts of a spontaneous life coming off her like the startled ghost of herself. But the trained eye sees in all the abrupt spectacle of frantic arms and legs outstretched on the bed, the specter of a feverish delirium that will take the body into a wild turn—eyes flashing, skirts flaring—lifting it off its feet forever and into a swirl of sensations that will thicken into a bitter paste on the patient's protesting tongue, until it chokes off every sound with the seal of mortar between bricks.

I see from the open doorway that the sickbed appears to have been set upon a heavy sea and the hapless daughter to have been swallowed into the belly of the whale that is bumping this furniture with its bowed back.

The bed jumps once. Then there is only the urgent

telegraphy of the metal feet against the floor, the sound of calamity swelling to fill the room with a concussion that might have resonated down a finely bored barrel.

Such was the shock that detonated Moertle's gunmetal eyes when I delivered the news of his daughter's demise. I spoke in my most deliberate voice of hypothesis and conclusion, mounting symptom upon symptom until the architecture of fatality rested upon his arched brow as an awesome edifice.

But my most patient numbering of the signs of illness was in fact only intended to gain time for myself to fill my own eyes with comprehension of what I saw before me. For as easily as I had read the symptoms of the disease on the daughter's small person, so it would be that much more difficult to tell the vast story of this Moertle's destruction from the appearance he presented to me there.

The injunction issued at the slaughterhouse gate must have struck him with the severity of the nail that held it above his questioning eyes. Perhaps at that moment he even heard the urgent ring of my voice in the bold-faced word—**QUARANTINE**—like the insect buzz already putting sticky legs on the membrane of an ear unable to distinguish the hearing from the motion of the head shaking it off. The word held him on its tether. His head hung on the heavy yoke that specified the terms of the quarantine: "No one shall enter under penalty of law."

He stamps his feet four times, blows through his nose,

nods toward the industrious hive of the sawblade, which he does not hear behind the split boards of the slaughterhouse gate. The narrow stall of his comprehension begins to hiss with the sound of a secret bodily expulsion. His sour breath squirms in the projectile of spit that he leaves sizzling on the curled leaf of the quarantine document. I would have needed my microscope to know whether the printed word could culture the germ that stained it.

And then there was not another sound to trample the slow, lumbering avowal that he released from his barred lips. I know everything he said, though he was speaking to himself. For me the words are like drops of water bellied with an image that makes them hang and sway and plop. And though the drops are as clear as eye-water, everything revealed in that glistening surface tension will burst like a bubble in the blink of an eye. Each ripening reflection falls at the moment of its fullest ingestion of imagery. So the vision of Moertle at the gate comes to my eyes with the urgency of a world awaiting destruction.

He had approached the locked doors of the slaughterhouse. He had read the terms of the injunction. He had departed.

Then he returns. But it is not to be a reconciliation with the leaded shot of print—**QUARANTINE**—which richocheted from his credulity.

He returns, yanking the leash of a tottering steer, aiming himself at the locked gate, the steel point of his concentration gleaming out in front of him like the knifepoint touching the center of his brain. The beast in tow is as dry and as brittle as any we find piled up on their own bones at the end of an empty street or lying on their sides, collecting sunlight in the declivity of their sunken hides and swimming with maggots. The shivering haunch is as thin as an edge of paper smacking the wind, and as sharp.

The gate is no obstacle for a man who has the key. The doors to the slaughterhouse flap wide wings against the lowering bosom of sunlight when they are opened. There is a rush of breath from the cellar darkness that has been pickling within. Under the wide lintel of the entrance-way, the hide of the steer is blown like still water into ripples over its back. A low moan is squeezed from the thinness of the animal girth as though Moertle's foot were playing the pedal of a sour organ. Simultaneously, the fumes of some furtive, gastric combustion rush upon Moertle as though he had trodden through a field of rotten vegetables in the darkness that is deepening with every step he takes into the empty building. But his sense of direction is unimpaired. Though he cannot find the breaker switch to make all before him visible, he has only to reach into the blind depths for the crucial implements of the task he has undertaken. He is confident that the darkness itself will conform to the shapes of his beckoning hands, like fistfuls of warm clay already wriggling to the rhythms of the labor he has in mind for them. That is how memory works.

So he accepts the blinding darkness as the torch of his other senses. He lights his lungs with the wick of a long breath. He thrusts his nose lanternlike out in front of each darkening step. He lets his ears burn to hear the paces of the animal in tow. For he has entered the long dark tunnel of pursuit that is as coiled with metamorphosis as the wet labyrinths of digestion.

179

The burnished light of reason is my only witness to what the darkness will not admit to sight.

Holding the shortened rope with one hand, Moertle finds the animal's jumping blood with the other. The warm haunch is still. But the pulse runs with a fury from under the long jaw to the depth of the chest, where he seizes a fold of loose skin as thin as the detachable tail of the elusive salamander panting safely under its rock. He marks the place with the strength of his twisting fingers. He will feel for it again as a bruise when he takes the animal's heart.

And from this moment, everything else seems to be swept along on the current he has traced with sensitive fingers to the place of the animal's heartbeat. Without a sense of direction, Moertle walks forward, finds the mouth of the narrow corridor that will swallow the animal whole and deliver it beneath the short metal bridge where he will be waiting.

There the blunt hammer weighs in Moertle's hand as though he were standing below his victim, submerged in a depth of rancid water rather than above, choking on the explosive air of the animal's fright. A coarse hair tickles his nose when Moertle takes his last breath. And then the contact of the hammerhead with the nodding skull begins a telepathic communication that will reverberate in every successive motion. It will carry Moertle toward an understanding of what pains his own head with such crystalline memory that he can execute in the dark what is usually possible—even for professional butchers—only under a strictly regulated wattage of searing light.

The handsaw flickers a little light to help him find his mark on the neck. The animal's head weighs with the shifting weight in Moertle's shoulders, permitting him to reach for it with aplomb when it drops from the tooth of the saw. The vibrations of the saw remain alive in Moertle's hand, though he has lost the instrument itself to the slippery mire at his feet. Then the head slips too on his greasy fingertips, and he is suddenly aware that the blackness all around him is merely a kindred sensation to the cold, ocular jelly where his thumb is stuck in an aghast socket of the animal eye.

He is glad to replace the head with the hook in his open hand. But the hook floats at his own eye level when he stands. It will not be lowered to the floor on its cold chain without a jolt from the electric generator, which will not warm to this enterprise.

Therefore Moertle must carry the weight of the carcass on his own back before it will dance above his head in the light of brandished cutlery. If the hook will not move, he will move to the hook. With the shoulder of beef draped over his shoulder, legs and hooves dangling the length of the human torso like straps of a preposterous knapsack where he takes his grip, Moertle is kneeling in the fetal position. It is the only position which gives the requisite leverage to catapult the headless carcass onto a point of steel as small and concentrated with invisible light as the undilated pupil of hate. But perhaps because this side of meat has already been shaved so close to the bone by shimmering blades of sunlight, Moertle's human frame, slightly canted forward, then seesawing in small movements beneath the length of its burden—somehow converting the inertia of the seesaw into a swift and tightly sprung vertical motion—is able to lift and project the ponderous motions of mammoth ani-

181

mal life, though the carcass weighs only as a phantom of its lumbering prairie existence.

Moertle's first exertion is ended. The splayed carcass swings from the gibbet by a tenuous noose of gristle pulled out from the hide like a bleached shirt collar. Wiping his brow, Moertle realizes that he is soaked through with the juices that gurgle around the pit of the fruit, even though he is only just now ready to pick up the knife and section the pulp.

Now the sensations of the spurting artery are coming from the sweaty hairs of his own chest, and the cloth of his trousers is bunching between his legs with every strenuous movement, as though he were perspiring with the animal's exertions, substituting his feeling for the animal's flesh.

"Memory is a leash tied at both ends. Nothing must be permitted to rest in its form of life or it is lost. The foot in the shut door is the one that fits the bruised slipper of our most miraculous transformations," are the words he spatters the walls with, working now in close quarters at the end of the alleyway, everything echoing against a metal trough where his feet are beginning to slip.

Long, curving and bitten with the toothmarks of a fiercer metal, the serrated knifeblade sends a shiver through the steer's underbelly when it is pierced, opening lips of conviviality that sigh, are licked with iridescence and finally gush forth with all the closely packed organs, like a bough struck off by lightning in the orchard, redolent of sugar and smoke and dripping long after it reaches the ground. Moertle's hands smear everything they touch. He no longer wants the knife handle and its solid grip on things. He would rather know the feathery kiss of the wounded lip on his elbows. He would rather know his hands buried deep inside the abdominal cavity and feeling for the root of things, the ducts knotty as chicken necks that he can snap between two fingers, the network of tubes branching without source or destination but deepening his entanglement until he cannot refuse the impulse to hold up a bowl-shaped organ—liver or third stomach—feeling for the buoying sensations of another world, puckering its lips, opening its gills, floating within.

And the uplifted chalice overflows, spilling gulping portions with each concussive syllable that Moertle projects, like a man heaving stones up the sides of a pit: ". . . rather . . . let everything be different . . . what is recognizable has already irreparably altered the eye persuaded of its familiarity . . . and the wistful sensations . . . the scattered . . . the restrung moments . . . when they are close as bees in the hive, then memory is a honeyed thing . . . but you cannot swallow it . . . its thickness occludes the throat . . . the tongue tells a different story then . . . the vanity of making whole pricks the eye as a shard from the mirror if you get too close . . . let the image seep from its cracks . . . not the mirror's . . . look again only if your face is hard enough to break that glass . . ."

And what was a welter of hiving life in the animal's belly is now a seething depth where Moertle's feet have sunk, making the lapping sounds of the ruined pier. But now the hatchet raised above his head—and despite the leather hood of darkness—shows that he has not found what he is looking for. So the head of the hatchet falls too, to the search.

The ribcage sounds like a wooden chest when it is broken open. Bones splinter too, intimations of light that prick the eager fingers guided along their curving paths. The animal lungs burst from their cage. The invasive touch of the atmosphere sweats the more intimate tissue beneath to a cluster of raisins clutched in a sodden fist. And far beneath the lungs, the heart twisted with its overgrowth of arteries like fattened leeches, is an indefatigable root that will not be pried loose until the hatchet's cold lip is sunk upon the thick shaft of the aorta. Finally, everything falls from the ribs of the carcass as dying fish to the unsteady bottom of the boat, slick, curving back into the air, briefly thrashing, slowly flattening beneath the pressing palm of darkness.

When the carcass is completely scooped out, and the long segmented spinal column and perpendicular shoulder bones are shining through a taut film of crimson saliva, then the slack hide and legs hang as if nailed to a crosstree, as if the armature of crucifixion were these very bones themselves from which the animal's life has always leapt at the world. Headless victim, its tail hung with weights to the floor, the carcass dangles without a shiver left like a curling hair to its chilly flank.

Moertle's upward gaze hangs too from the only light dredged out of this long immersion in darkness, winking from the tip of the steel hook. Now, and by that fiercely honed light, I can see what has been obscured by the feverish activity of this slaughter. I can see that the slow uncovering of layer upon layer of membranous tissue, which had first appeared to be the compunction of a meticulous search, was in fact only the brusque clearing of space for what is now fully discovered and restless to be free in all the tensile anatomy of Moertle's own body.

He stands on the last rung of a stepladder. It must have been there all along like the cliff edge on a moonless night. He stands as if ready to embrace the full length of the stripped carcass or else to receive it with its ribs splayed out like the flared coat of the exhibitionist. It offers only the pale stiffness of the hook, lower than eye level to Moertle's eye, but pointing up.

His is the grey fish mouth poised for the silver hook. He sees nothing else because he has deliberately hung the drying steer. He has beheaded the carcass. He has split the hide and carved out the walls of the animal girth only to make a place for himself there (especially where the animal head roars its absence), to replace the horns, the shocked eyes and rippling nostrils with the frenzied mask of his own fright. Moertle wants to hang his own head on the hook. And because he has relieved the carcass of the weight that hung within it like a second life, he believes that the hook will support them both.

Only a gentle kick at the ladder, a fanciful trapeze motion of flying arms and legs to cross three steps of pitch air, head pointed high and he will feel the frozen tip of the hook rising in the back of his own throat stiff with the alarum of a screaming tongue.

But Moertle has forgotten that the darkness is a cloak thrown over the scene of all such imaginings. So, with his head thrust out and bowing into the mouth of destruction, he merely falls upon the shoulder of the carcass and does not even whisper to the hook in passing.

The glancing blow is enough to cause the hook to bite completely through the gristly collar where it held its prey, landing the carcass on top of the man and both into the pit of offal. The naked hook swings above them like a windblown moon.

The contact of the two bodies resounds with a splash. The sound is indistinguishable from the motion with which Moertle spews from the stagnant center of the well, drenched in outrage, speechless because his mouth is clamped upon a crapulous curd, holding it with his teeth so it doesn't touch his tongue, but unable to propel it over the squeamish lip without a nudge from the back of his throat. He cannot use his hands quickly enough to wring out the wetness binding him in his own clothes. And the frantic movements that have put him unsteadily on his feet and tipped him forward in the depth of darkness until he is swimming furiously toward the light of the open door—it has dilated over his shoulder since he entered—exhale the final breath of the animal's existence, because with each step forward Moertle feels the animal breath suspiring over his skin with the sour stench of digesting grasses, spoiled hays, fermented pollen, pursuing him into the open corral on wider and wider wings of ghostly odor.

Moving in full stride out of the slaughterhouse gate, Moertle is leaving bloody footprints like boiled kidneys in the sunlight. Yet they are camouflaged over an expanse of ground already blooming with crimson flowers, sprouted so closely to the earth that it might be soaked with them. Had Moertle eyes for anything but the path beating down my door, he would have lost them amid the cresting grasses grown long enough to wave at a passing fugitive on the road, but thrown back like a wet head of hair over the aroused body of land he crossed.

Moertle touches me when he sees me. He is trying to pinch himself out of the dream by getting a better grip on his surroundings. He is smearing my clinical lapel as

186

though I had been brusquely pulling the heads of chickens across my chest. He is fairly bursting with the color he imparts to me. It is in his clotted hair no less than on his bobbing dimples. It is dripping from the inside of his shirt cuff no less than from the pinched corners of his eyes. He is himself the picked fruit already crushed between impatient fingers where they are breaking it off its stems.

Knowing full well everything he had to tell, I waited to hear it from his own lips.

"The doctor is dead, not so fat a man that he couldn't swell to bursting from the fever that was like an expanding gas. It had crouched inside him, the sweaty genie of his own fatness blowing on the cork of the bottle to free itself. The heat of the fever rose over him, stroking his head solicitously until he could not refuse to meet his own shadow on the hard ground. It could not be said that the ground tasted good where it broke his teeth back against the tongue, forcing him to swallow the contents of the smashed flowerpot. Contagion is a seed planted between two fingers; let the pot be big enough for the seed to grow."

The clacking lips conjure the resonant enamel of painted teeth masticating everything that comes into the wooden mouth, until the warming hinge-pin puckers like an enflamed tonsil at the back of the throat, the jawline cracks, shivers sideways, sprays a penumbra of discolored paint chips. And the levered tongue snaps off against the roof of the mouth—it will not get another lift—falls back

187

to jam the mechanism of the throat seizing up the oper-
ator's hand in its turn.

The lever comes loose in the hand that moves it.

I have smashed the wooden boy's head without a
splinter to tell me his pain. But the tongue is still jumping on its string inside my own head. Throwing the
voice.

"Hoof and mouth is a disease of four-legged creatures."

Though many have died, yet there will be no end of
contagion. Because the audible lip is connected to the air,
which becomes a blanket thrown wide over everything in
sight. And what pulls at one corner is felt at the opposite
end as an impossible longing.

Ventriloquism is like this:

You hold your tongue stiff as a wand so that its movements are more magical with every word it touches. Your
bite is rigid. You must keep the air coming like blocks of
stone on the stooped back of your laboring throat, building a monumental deceit. For when your mouth is stone-
still, though everything in it is thrashing the green violence of the lizard's tail, your voice will move across another's lips, a ripple spreading over the illusory surface of
everything your audience can see.

When we are talking to each other, we are always
speaking over water, moving other faces with our breath
until the imping recognition comes that they are our own
trembling faces below us, and we are chest high in the
flow of things.

We are children who never grow old, preserved in the

188

loss of the face that washes away beneath our gaze. And if it does not pass away, blow harder.

Blow harder. And I must have more breath. What there is to say requires a brimming lung, a diaphragm like a trampoline.

The picture that hovers in the moist eye does not last. Therefore let the eyelid fall a remorseless blade. And if that picture smuggles itself into the belly of a shedding tear, let that tear run down your face. Swallow it out of the cupped corner of your mouth. Learn to tell the story so you will forget the picture it imprints. Make everything pass over your lips and from that precipice you may leap to safety.

I am a ventriloquist for love. But the man I saw doing it the first time did it for money. They brought a chair so that he could put his knees up for the doll to sit. I couldn't tell if the hat they were passing through the crowd fit the one head or the other. Its proportions changed so in each hand that touched it on its clinking way. And neither the man slouched in his chair nor the stiff-backed doll spoke at first. But the gawkers who had heard tell of what was to come—they heard it at dusty crossroads and on abandoned train platforms—filled the air with the expectation of a profound bewilderment. Someone began to twirl a stick with red and white ribbons on it as if they had just remembered a holiday. Someone stood by with a snare drum at the ready and hissing like a snake coiled in its basket.

The seated man seemed to grow smaller in his baggy trainman's uniform as he started to work, shrinking in proportion to the movements he prodded the doll with. The doll's head rotated sideways. It crossed its legs. It

189

held up an open palm. When at last it happened, no one noticed that the sagging trainman had given his eyes with the first words he gave to the clacking puppet. The wooden lids slapped open wide enough to swallow, showing pupils that were red as any hungry mouth. The drummer forgot to roll his drum. The beribboned stick flew into a dust cloud at someone's feet. Men with their hats on removed them and squelched them under their arms. Women gathered their skirts more tightly, since they could not tell where the voice was loose in the air around them. No one breathed in.

It was a voice cinched tightly around our ears, compelling attention, prickly like someone holding a fork to your naked back. Because it was a desperate plea.

Though it was unmistakably the aged trainman who had withered like a dying vine against the lattice back of the chair—blind and mute in this decrepitude—it was the spry boy buoyed up on his knee who told a story of bereavement.

The boy said he was being eaten alive. The life was breathed out of his lungs by the man who held him in a fatherly embrace. Everything he had to say was sucked out of him when he said it. Even these words he said pulled a long thread from his gut so that it wriggled like a fish on the line. The boy called himself a broken bone, as if the bone could contemplate the dog's tongue burrowing at its marrow-laden cusp. For him, to speak was to endure the crunch of teeth not his own, to be wrapped in a tongue that tasted his own demise, to salivate from all the perspiring joints of his sundering frame.

Though it appeared that the trainman had slipped silently beneath an abeyant surface—not even the knowledgeable wink of an air bubble in his wake—and though his eyes were still, his lips were sealed, a ravenous smile appeared across the eclipsed moon of his face, bright as a bared tooth.

It was true. He was the eater. He was eating the soft tissue of the life he proffered with his own controlled breath. He was following a plan of digestion that he had studied well and that he held in readiness like the whittled bone of poise at the back of his clutched throat. He ate with the remorseless reflexes of a long and serious regimen of practice.

You practice, too. Say, "My Moertle, my Papa." Let your winged face hover closer to the watery surface. See yourself there. Stillness pervades the smoothness. Though you may not move your lips, yet you must project enough air to stir the surface with a stick. Your face will be your dummy. So concentrate on the rigid mask reflected beneath your gaze, and if it does not move, blow harder.